Fear of Falling

To Wild at Heart fans, who love reading almost as much as they love animals

Acknowledgments
Special thanks to Cathy East Dubowski; thanks also to Kimberly Michels, D.V.M.;
Kiddy McCarthy; Susan Dickert and Barzalt; Madison Equine Clinic; Dan and
Judy Lynch; and Troxel, for allowing a Troxel equestrian riding helmet to
appear on the front cover.

Please visit our web site at: www.garethstevens.com
For a free color catalog describing Gareth Stevens Publishing's list of high-quality
books and multimedia programs, call 1-800-542-2595 (USA) or 1-800-387-3178
(Canada). Gareth Stevens Publishing's fax: (414) 332-3567.

Library of Congress Cataloging-in-Publication Data

Anderson, Laurie Halse.
   Fear of falling / by Laurie Halse Anderson.
       p. cm. — (Wild at Heart)
       Summary: Twelve-year-old David has conflicting feelings when his father, who taught
him to ride the horses he loves so much, returns to spend Thanksgiving Day with the family
after being gone for a year.
       ISBN 0-8368-3255-8 (lib. bdg.)
       [1. Family problems—Fiction. 2. Fathers and sons—Fiction. 3. Horsemanship—Fiction.
4. Horses—Fiction. 5. Thanksgiving Day—Fiction.] I. Title.
PZ7.A54385Fd   2003
[Fic]—dc21   2002036517

This edition first published in 2003 by
Gareth Stevens Publishing
A World Almanac Education Group Company
330 West Olive Street, Suite 100
Milwaukee, WI 53212 USA

First published by Pleasant Company Publications, Middleton, Wisconsin.
Original © 2001 by Laurie Halse Anderson. Illustration and design © 2001
by Pleasant Company.

American Girl® and Wild at Heart™ are trademarks of Pleasant Company.

Cover Photography: Brian Malloy
Newspaper Clipping Photography: Jamie Young

Photo Credits: page 106—© Kit Houghton Photography/CORBIS; page 107—photo
by Debra Baumann; © Kit Houghton Photography/CORBIS; page 108—© Michael S.
Yamashita/CORBIS (detail); © Christie's Images/CORBIS; page 109—photo by Debra
Baumann; page 110—© Michael St. Maur Sheil/CORBIS

Although Ambler, Pennsylvania, is a real town (a wonderful town!), the setting, characters,
and events that take place in this book are all fictional. Any similarity to real persons,
living or dead, is coincidental and not intended by the author. This book is not intended as
a substitute for your veterinarian. Your vet is the best source of health advice for your pet.

Printed in the United States of America

1 2 3 4 5 6 7 8 9 07 06 05 04 03

Fear of Falling

Laurie Halse Anderson

Gareth Stevens Publishing
A WORLD ALMANAC EDUCATION GROUP COMPANY

ONE

It's happening again.

I'm riding a horse, a big one. He's fast, powerful, and a little headstrong. A horse that's easy to admire but hard to ride.

I check my seat, make sure I'm balanced. People are calling my name, but I can't understand what they're trying to tell me.

The horse and I head straight for the first jump. *Come on, come on, come on.* I lean forward, and we're up, we're flying . . .

Then that jolt of connecting with the ground again. We made it—but my heart is pounding faster than the horse's hooves.

The second jump is higher. *Maybe we ought to skip it.* But the horse picks up speed and heads straight for the jump. He's already decided we're taking it.

Approach, leap, *fly* . . . I'm amazed when we actually clear it.

My horse canters steadily. I start to relax. Then I see what's next—and get chills from head to toe. This third jump is impossibly high. No horse could ever clear a jump like that. Desperately I pull back on the reins.

The horse won't listen to me. I can feel his excitement, the tension in his muscles that tells me he's going for it.

What, are you crazy? I pull with all my weight on one rein to turn him away from the jump, but the horse totally ignores me. Instead, he takes off at full gallop, and I panic. If I jump off now, I'll break my neck for sure. But if he tries that jump, we're both goners.

And then it's too late to do anything but hang on as his front feet leave the ground. We're defying gravity, we're *really* flying, and for a moment I believe that this incredible horse and I are going to make it. His forelegs clear the jump—

Suddenly I hear a loud *thunk* as his back hooves hit the crossbar, and there's a sickening lurch. I close my eyes tight. Then we're falling, falling . . .

Someone screams my name: *"Da-vi-i-i-d . . ."*

It's going to hurt so bad when I hit the ground—

"Da-vid . . . *David!*"

The next thing I know, I'm lying flat on my back at a twisted angle. But the ground doesn't feel hard. Maybe I'm so badly injured I can't feel anything.

"Earth to David!"

I fight to open my eyes.

"David, you idiot, wake *up!*" My big brother, Brian, shoves me so hard he nearly knocks me out of bed.

I sit up, panting, coated in a cold sweat.

"Mom says you've got two minutes before you have to leave for the stables," Brian says.

Leave for the stables . . . But the horse . . . For a minute I'm swimming between two worlds.

Brian shoves his face in front of mine. "The parade's today, dork. Get up, will ya? Mom says I can't leave till I get you out of bed!"

I collapse back on the scrunched-up covers. OK, it was just a dream—but not just any dream. It's a dream I've had before. A dream I hate.

So why do I keep having it?

Suddenly Brian's words sink in, and I bolt up again. "The parade!"

My brother stands in the doorway and looks at me like I'm a lost cause. "OK, you're up now. I'm outta here."

I fling off my covers. It's Saturday—the Thanksgiving parade through Ambler is today! I'm riding in it for the first time, with Mr. Quinn, Zoe Hopkins, and some of the other kids from Quinn's Stables. I've been waiting for this day for weeks, and now it's finally here.

I can get ready fast when I need to. I jump out of bed, throw on the clothes I laid out last night (Mr. Quinn wants us to look sharp), chew on my toothbrush for about three seconds, then comb both hands through my hair as I pound down the stairs.

When I hit the floor, I glance out the window by the front door. Did they leave yet? Nope, Dr. Mac's van is still parked in the driveway at Wild at Heart, the animal clinic across the street from my house. I volunteer at the clinic with some other kids when I have free time. Dr. Mac—her real name is Dr. J.J. MacKenzie—is the veterinarian who runs the clinic.

I yank open the door and peer out. Nobody's in the van yet. Good, I have time to grab a bite.

Heading into the kitchen, I hear Mom and my kid sister, Ashley, arguing again. What is it this time—clothes? Mutilated Barbie hair? Whether she's allowed to go out in public wearing those fake tattoos all her friends are wearing?

At the table, Mom has set out vitamins, orange juice, skim milk, and some kind of nutritional fiber cereal. I sigh. We never have anything fun for breakfast, like Pop-Tarts. Sometimes I think it's Mom's way of trying to make us safe before she sends us off into the scary world. As if Flintstones vitamins will protect us from the Big Bad Wolf.

But I shouldn't be too hard on her. I think she's still getting used to being a single mom and feels bad about leaving us to go off to work each day.

I pour myself a bowl of little brown buds that look an awful lot like mouse droppings. I'm supposed to *eat* these? I give Mom a suffering look.

That's when I notice Ashley is wearing her favorite purple sundress.

Mom's holding a pair of jeans, a turtleneck, and a thick sweater. "Ashley, be reasonable," she says. "It's the end of November and you live in Pennsylvania, not Florida."

Ashley stubbornly shakes her head. "I have to wear my dress."

"You'll freeze!" Mom says.

"No, I won't. I like cold."

Mom shakes her head, but I can tell she's trying not to laugh. "I doubt that, young lady. Now, come on. People will think I'm a bad mother."

Ashley shrugs. She's only five. She doesn't care what other grown-ups think about her mother.

While they go round and round, I bolt down my cereal and button my shirt. Brian's totally oblivious, standing up at the counter guzzling milk straight out of the carton.

"Brian!" Mom exclaims. "How many times have I asked you to use a glass for your milk?"

"Sorry, Mom." Brian takes a final swig, then wipes his mouth on his sleeve and puts the carton back in the fridge.

I glance at Mom. I can't believe she lets him get away with stuff like that. She's not that easy on me. Maybe she's given up on him, since he's sixteen and is gone half the time anyway.

Besides, she's got her hands full this morning with Ashley and her sundress. Ashley loves that dress more than anything. Dad sent it to her for her birthday.

"Ashley, I'm going to count to five—"

"But Mom," Ashley says, looking up at our mother with those big blue eyes that are so much like Dad's. "I have to keep it on all the time. For when Daddy comes."

"Daddy who?" Brian cracks.

Ashley folds her arms and frowns at Brian as if

he's the little kid and she's the one who's six feet tall. "You know Daddy who! *Our* Daddy. Daddy Charlie Hutchinson!"

Brian just rolls his eyes and shrugs into his jacket.

Mom's face closes up like a shade pulled down. I know she's thinking what I'm thinking. Dad called last week out of the blue and said he was coming for Thanksgiving, and now Ashley's so excited. Because she still believes in things. Things like the Easter bunny and the tooth fairy—and Dad's promises.

But I've heard his promises before. Ever since Dad took the transfer to Texas last year, we haven't seen him at all. Not once. At first I believed Dad when he said we were only going to be apart for a little while, till he got settled in the job. Then we'd figure things out, he said.

I never really understood what we had to figure out, exactly. It seemed simple—either come back home or take us out to Texas with him. Yet somehow neither of those things happened.

Brian acts like he doesn't care at all, like he's too busy to notice Dad's gone. He never even mentions Dad. But that's partly because Brian's hardly ever here anymore. After Dad left, Brian went out and got a job at the multiplex at the mall, and his job seems to take up most of his free time.

And Mom? She doesn't say much about Dad anymore either, but that doesn't mean she isn't thinking about him. I want to ask her what she's thinking, but how does a twelve-year-old boy ask his mother for the lowdown on her marriage? I mean, I still have trouble talking to her about my math grades!

So we all just go on pretending nothing's wrong and waiting for Dad to come home . . . with Ashley running downstairs to look out the window every morning, as if she thinks Santa is going to leave Dad on our doorstep or something.

"Don't hold your breath, Ashley," I mutter.

"Why not?" she asks, then immediately starts holding her breath, making a big show of how fat her cheeks are. That's the kind of kid she is. Say "Don't step in a puddle," and she jumps in with both feet to find out why.

Mom looks annoyed. "Ashley, stop that. Do you want to turn blue? Ashley—" Mom gives up and starts to load the dishwasher. "I guess she'll breathe when she needs to."

A horn beeps outside, and Brian peers out the kitchen window. "It's the guys, Mom. Gotta go."

"Brian—wait!" Mom says. "You haven't eaten anything."

Brian digs into the cereal box for a handful of those bran buds, shoving them into his mouth as he heads out the door. "Yum!" he shouts over his shoulder. "You're a great cook, Mom! See you guys at the parade." And he's gone.

Mom shakes her head and turns back to the dishes.

"I think it's wrong to let Ashley go on believing Dad's going to show up for Thanksgiving," I mutter to Mom as I scrape back my chair and stand up.

"David!" Mom whispers through clenched teeth, sending me a look that says, *Watch what you say in front of Ashley.*

I shrug and carry my bowl to the sink. "Well, you know it's true," I whisper back. "Dad's not too good about keeping promises anymore."

Mom sighs heavily. I guess she knows that even better than I do. "All right, David," she says quietly. "I'm skeptical, too. But I'm going to keep an open mind, and I want you to do the same, at least around Ashley."

"OK, I guess." I head into the hall to get my jacket. Inside the coat closet, Ashley's backpack is half open on the floor. There's a drawing poking out, done with colored markers. The drawing is of two goofy-eyed stick people. One is big with yellow hair. The smaller one is holding the big one's hand. Across the top it says, "I lov yu Dady."

Suddenly I fight back a choked feeling in my throat. I used to have the same hope about Dad that Ashley does. I mean, we're his kids, his family. How could he leave us and not come back?

But the days turned into weeks, and the weeks into months. First the phone calls stopped. He was never good at writing letters, but he did e-mail us sometimes. Then even the e-mails stopped coming. Mom hasn't said anything specific, but money is so tight now that I sometimes wonder if he's stopped sending her checks, too.

Thinking about Dad gives me that falling feeling—the one I have in the dream. *Don't go there,* I tell myself. *Just forget about it.*

A horn honks in the driveway, and I yank open the front door. Dr. Mac leans her head out of the van and waves. "Come on, David. Let's go!"

Yes! It's time to ride.

"See ya, Mom," I shout, then slam the door and leave all that other stuff behind.

When we arrive at Quinn's Stables, Brenna and Sunita are already there. Maggie, Zoe, and I pile out of Dr. Mac's van and run to meet them, laughing and sharing high fives. We're totally pumped up for the parade.

Guys don't usually hang out with four girls, but this is different. They're all volunteers at Wild at Heart, same as me. Dr. Mac is Maggie and Zoe's grandmother. She asked for our help once when the clinic was swamped with a bunch of sick, starving puppies from a puppy mill. We did a pretty good job saving the puppies and tracking down the sleazy dog breeder who was selling them, so Dr. Mac asked us to be regular volunteers at the clinic.

We get to help out with real medical stuff, too—checkups, shots, even emergencies. Of course, we still have to do the chores, such as cleaning cages and stocking supply closets. But it's worth it to be helping the animals.

I race the girls to the barn and go straight to check on my favorite horse. "Hey, Trickster!" I call out to him, and his head pops over the stall door.

Mr. Quinn and I have been working with Trickster for months to get him ready for the parade today. I scratch behind his ears, and he nickers. He's the best.

Zoe comes up behind me. "How's Trickster doing?" she asks. She's the only one of the girls who's into horses as much as I am. She used to live in Manhattan with her actress mother and went to some fancy summer riding camp. She really knows her stuff when it comes to riding.

"Trickster's great," I say. "Aren't you, boy?"

Zoe strokes his nose, frowning. "Think he'll go into the trailer without a fuss?"

"I hope so." I first met Trickster when Mr. Quinn brought him into the stables back in the spring. Trickster's leg got injured when his horse trailer was hit on the highway. Dr. Mac treated his leg, and it was a while before he could carry a rider. But almost worse was how the accident hurt Trickster's spirit—how terrified he became of trailers.

Lately Mr. Quinn and I have been reintroducing him to the trailer v-e-r-y s-l-o-w-l-y. Hey, I can relate—I know what it's like to do something scary. Like riding a horse over a jump, for example.

"Good morning," Dr. Mac says cheerfully to the horses as she enters the barn. "How are all you beauties today?"

"Raring to go!" Mr. Quinn says with a smile.

Dr. Mac checks the parade horses over, and then we begin loading the horses into the trailers that will carry them to the starting point of the parade. It's not far into town, but with the traffic and crowds, Mr. Quinn feels the horses will be calmer and safer in the trailers. He really loves his horses. That's one reason he and my dad were always such good friends—they shared a love of horses.

It was Dad who first taught me to ride. Now that Dad's gone, Mr. Quinn has been teaching me. When Mr. Quinn first started giving me jumping lessons, I was excited, but now I'm not so sure I'm ready.

"Here we go, David. It's D-day—let's see how Trickster loads," says Mr. Quinn.

I lead Trickster to the trailer, talking in a calm, low voice to reassure him.

Trickster hesitates, but only for a moment, and then he walks up the ramp into the trailer without a second glance. Yes!

I turn to Mr. Quinn. "He did it!"

He winks at me and nods. "Looks like all your hard work paid off, huh?"

I grin. Mr. Quinn doesn't hand out praise easily, especially to me. I had a little trouble convincing him I was a responsible kid a while back. But he's been patient with me.

While the other horses are being loaded, I notice

a new horse, very tall, charcoal gray with a silver mane. He's awesome!

I walk over to one of the stable hands. "Hey, Joe. Who's the new horse?"

"Oh, him." Joe puts his hands on his hips and shakes his head in admiration. "His name is King's Shadow—he's a jumper. A real beaut, huh? He's a new boarder, just brought in yesterday."

"He's amazing," I say. I stretch out my hand, palm down, to let King's Shadow smell me.

Over near the trailers, I catch Mr. Quinn watching me—or is it King's Shadow he's watching? When our eyes meet, he quickly glances away with an odd look on his face. *What's that about?*

Dr. Mac calls us. "Let's go, kids. We don't want to be late."

I forget about Mr. Quinn's strange look. I'm going to ride Trickster in a parade!

TWO

Dr. Mac says the Ambler Thanksgiving parade is "old-fashioned America." Everyone from miles around comes to town for the event. Excitement is in the air, and everybody's in a holiday spirit. Families line the streets, fathers holding their kids high up on their shoulders.

Families. The thought is like a punch in the gut. Holidays are supposed to bring families together. I think of Dad and try not to search the crowd for him. If he shows up, he shows up. If he doesn't . . .

I shrug. I'm too old to think like Ashley—to think that I can blow out birthday candles and my wish will come true just because I want it to.

In the parking lot behind the grocery store, we unload the horses from the trailers, backing them out one by one. Trickster does just fine. I'm so proud of him! I give him a quick final brushing. His chest-nut coat is a rich reddish brown, and it shines in the sunlight. As usual, his long forelock flops over his eyes. I smile—he likes his bangs in his eyes, just like me. Carefully I comb his forelock into the center of his forehead, and he shakes it right back into his eyes. He's playful—that's how he got the name Trickster.

The horses are used to being around people for riding lessons and horse shows. Still, we're careful to talk softly and keep them calm as we saddle up. The excitement grows as we take our places in the parade.

"Sunita and I are going to head over to the booth now," Dr. Mac says. They've set up a Wild at Heart table, where they'll hand out information about pet care and vaccinations. She waves to us. "We'll be watching!"

Up ahead I spot Maggie with a bunch of her friends from school. They've all got their dogs, and they plan to entertain the crowd with obedience tricks. Maggie has her big old basset hound, Sherlock Holmes, on a leash. He's not exactly the fastest dog in the west, but Maggie's got him so well trained, I know he'll put on a good show.

Brenna is darting around taking pictures of

everything. She's really into photography, and she's hoping that one of her photographs will get printed in the newspaper.

I put my left foot in the stirrup and swing up into Trickster's saddle. Wow, what a view! Trickster is fifteen hands high. Since a hand equals four inches, that means Trickster is five feet tall at his withers, where his neck and back meet. So I'm way above the crowd! I can see everything . . . Girl Scouts wearing reindeer antlers, a city fire truck all polished up and decorated with bunting, the high-school marching band playing holiday tunes.

"Brenna!" I call down to her. "You should be up here. You can see almost the whole parade!"

She snaps a picture of me, then looks up from behind the lens. "Yeah, right. And which hand would I hold the reins in while I'm focusing the camera?"

She has me there.

Suddenly, off in the crowd, the sunlight hits a shock of blond hair—a man craning his neck—and my heart leaps. *Dad!*

But when the man turns, I realize it's not him, and I feel like an idiot. *This is no sappy holiday movie*, I remind myself. I can't help wondering how Ashley's going to feel when Dad doesn't show up for Thanksgiving dinner.

How will *I* feel?

Trickster snorts and steps sideways. I guess I was squeezing his sides too tightly. "Sorry, boy," I whisper, patting his neck. He can probably tell I'm feeling tense. Dad says horses always know what we're thinking and feeling, even when we don't know ourselves.

"*David!*"

"Huh?"

"Quit daydreaming," Zoe says with a grin. "The parade's starting."

"Hey, I'm ready!" I tell myself to forget about Dad. Because right now I'm doing my favorite thing in the world—riding Trickster.

As the parade gets under way, I start to relax and have a good time. Being in a parade is so cool! I scan the sea of faces lining the sidewalk and spot Brian with some of his buddies from the multiplex.

"Hey, David, nice wheels!" Brian calls out, shooting me the thumbs-up sign.

I can't help breaking into a grin, thankful that he didn't shout out some snotty insult to impress his friends. You just never know what a big brother is going to do when he's out in public.

Rachel, the cute girl who sits in front of me in

science class, waves at me like I'm some kind of celebrity. "I love your horse!" she shouts. She and her friends fall all over themselves, giggling.

"David! You're blushing!" Zoe teases from her horse, a tall bay named Claiborne.

I duck my head and turn toward the other side of the street, pretending that I have to wave an equal amount on both sides. Is there any way to make your face un-blush? But I have to admit I love getting all this attention. I feel like a movie star.

Suddenly the fire truck up ahead blares its siren, startling me—and my horse. Trickster spooks and skitters sideways, catching me off balance. I clutch the saddle as my legs fly out of the stirrups. It feels like I'm going to fall, but I regain my balance just in time and quickly bring Trickster under control.

Behind us, Claiborne snorts. Turning to check on Zoe, I see Claiborne rear, his forelegs pawing the air. Zoe's face is white. I've never seen her look scared on a horse before.

"Hang on, Zoe!" I shout.

Zoe grabs a handful of mane and leans forward into Claiborne's neck, her legs tight against the horse's flanks. Just as suddenly, Claiborne drops back down, his hooves clattering on the asphalt, and Zoe loses her grip and tumbles to the street.

"Zoe!" I cry, reining Trickster to a stop, terrified that she'll be trampled by Claiborne's hooves. She needs help, but I'm not sure what to do; I've got my own horse to control. Just as I'm about to dismount, Mr. Quinn rushes up and grabs Claiborne's reins.

"Are you all right?" I call down to Zoe.

She stands up slowly, brushing off her arms. "I think so!" she says breathlessly. She looks at her elbow. It's badly scraped.

"Mr. Quinn," I call out. "Zoe's bleeding!"

Mr. Quinn glances at her arm and pulls out a bandanna for her to wrap around the scrape. "You need to go to the first-aid station, Zoe," he tells her. "I'll take care of Claiborne." He points out a booth with a red cross on it. "Can you make it there on your own?"

Zoe nods, but I can tell she's disappointed about not finishing the parade.

"I'm sorry, Zoe," I tell her.

She shrugs. "No biggie. Don't worry about me. You go ahead. Have fun!"

I wave good-bye to Zoe and continue on with the other riders. We're past the shops now, and both sides of the street are lined with tables. The firefighters have a safety exhibit, and the 4-H club is signing up new members. When we pass the Wild at Heart booth, Sunita and Dr. Mac are so busy handing out pamphlets about vaccinations and spaying and neutering that they don't even see us ride by. Dr. Mac must be really pleased. She likes it when people want to learn about being responsible pet owners.

I can smell hot dogs and sausages grilling. That means we're near the end. My stomach rumbles. *Man, am I hungry!* Maybe I can sneak in a little snack without Mom seeing. Her health-food kick is starving me to death!

We round a corner, and up ahead I spot a little girl in a purple sundress waving wildly in my direction. Don't tell me Mom actually let Ashley wear that dress! As I draw closer, I see she's got jeans and a sweater on under the dress. Looks like she and Mom worked out a deal. I have to hand it to Mom— how many mothers would let their daughter go out in public dressed like that?

"You're one block from the end," Mom calls as I ride up. "Come join us for lunch after you're done."

"Mom packed a picnic!" Ashley shouts. "With pickles!" The people around her chuckle. That's my sister for you—never a dull moment.

"OK, Ash, I'll be there as soon as I can," I call down.

At the end of the parade, we circle back to the trailers and load the horses. Then I meet Mom and Ashley at the park for lunch.

"One of the booths had the cutest goat," Ashley says, sucking on a pickle. "It had long curly hair. Can we go pet it?"

Long curly hair on a goat? This I have to see. "All right if we go, Mom?"

Mom nods. "Just walk Ashley home when you're done."

"Can I feed my sandwich crusts to the goat?" Ashley asks as we pack up the food.

"Well, we can ask the owner if it's OK." I take Ashley's hand so I don't lose her in the crowd, and we start back up Main Street. Now that the parade is over, the booths are mobbed.

Suddenly Ashley looks worried. "But what if the goat bites me?"

"Don't worry. Goats don't have any teeth on their upper jaw, so they can't hurt you," I tell her. "Besides, I'm sure it's a nice goat, or they wouldn't have brought it here."

"Look, David, there it is!" Ashley points, and through the crowd I spot a small white goat in a wire pen. It has long curly hair, just as Ashley said. In fact, it looks almost like a sheep, except for the narrow horns curving back from its head. Suddenly it bleats. I wonder if it's scared of all the people.

The table in front of the goat pen displays hand-made posters about spinning and knitting with mohair wool. A woman in a long skirt demonstrates a spinning wheel, while a girl who looks about ten years old hands out wool samples.

I approach the girl. "Hi—is it all right if we pet your goat?"

The girl nods. "Sure. She's real soft because she's an Angora. She's a little noisy, but don't worry, she's very friendly. Her name is Sabrina. If you call her, she'll come right up to you."

"Will she eat my crusts?" Ashley holds up her chewed sandwich remains.

The girl smiles. "She probably would, but she needs a special diet, so they wouldn't be good for her."

"A diet? Is she too fat?" Ashley asks.

The girl shakes her head and laughs. "No, but to make all that nice long hair, she has to eat special high-protein pellets. If she fills up on your sand-wich, she might not eat her dinner."

Ashley nods knowingly. "That's just what my mom tells *me!*"

As Ashley and I walk over to the pen, the goat

bleats again. She's got her head poking through the fence, watching us.

"Here, Sabrina," Ashley calls, but the goat doesn't move. No wonder: as we come up to her, I can see that the wire fence is caught behind her horns, and she can't pull her head back through.

"Let's get you unstuck," I say to the goat. Holding a horn, I gently twist her head, then slowly back it through the square of fence. Suddenly Sabrina squirms and bleats again. "Hold still, I'm trying to help!" I mutter. "There!"

The second her horns are free of the fence, Sabrina jerks her head back and bolts across the pen.

Ashley trots around the pen after Sabrina, who stops and lets Ashley pet her. "Ooh, look at all her fancy curls everywhere. And her white eyelashes!" my sister marvels. "Hey David, look—the poor goat is crying. Do you think she's sad that she doesn't get to eat my crusts?"

"Animals don't cry, Ashley."

"Then how come there are tears coming out of her eye?"

What on earth is Ashley babbling about this time? I go over to the goat. Sure enough, tears are running out of Sabrina's left eye and down her furry cheek. The eyelids look squinty, too.

"See?" Ashley's lower lip trembles. She's about to cry herself. "We have to comfort her!" She reaches her arms through the fence, trying to give Sabrina a hug.

"We have to find out what's wrong with her eye," I reply, peering more closely. Suddenly Sabrina shakes her head, and I catch a flash of red on her neck. *What was that?*

I pull apart the long woolly ringlets. On the skin of her neck, I find a red cut about two inches long, with blood oozing out. It was practically hidden in all her hair.

I go back and examine the place in the pen where Sabrina was stuck. Where the fence is nailed to the post, there's a sharp piece of wire sticking out with a tangle of long white hairs stuck on it. Sabrina must have scratched herself when she yanked her head back through the fence.

I tell Ashley to stay put, and then I run back to the girl at the table to borrow some paper towels and a cell phone. I hope Dr. Mac has her pager switched on.

A few minutes later, while we're waiting for Dr. Mac to arrive, the girl and her mother look at Sabrina's injuries. The neck cut looks terrible now, with blood dripping all down the goat's white hair.

I press a wad of paper towels firmly onto the cut, like a pressure bandage, to stop the bleeding. But it's the scratched eye that worries me the most.

Ashley is trying to be brave, but as we wait for Dr. Mac, she begins to sob. The girl, whose name is Julie, cries a little, too, and her mom looks anxious. Only Sabrina seems calm and unconcerned.

When Dr. Mac arrives, she puts a drop of anesthetic into Sabrina's eye to numb it, and then a drop of yellow-green stain. Then she examines the eye with her ophthalmoscope, which looks just like the kind people doctors use to check their patients' eyes. Peering through the scope, she rolls back the goat's eyelid and shines a little beam of light all around. Goats have funny eyes, yellow with a flat pupil shaped like a bar.

"There's a scratch on the cornea," Dr. Mac announces. "The stain makes it show up. That's why this eye is tearing so badly."

"Will she be all right?" Julie whispers.

"I think so. I'll give you some antibiotic ointment to use so the eye doesn't become infected, and I'll recheck her in a few days. The eye should heal up nicely on its own."

Next Dr. Mac rinses the neck wound with saline from a squeeze bottle. She examines the wound closely, frowning. "This cut's rather deep. It'll have to be stitched up."

Dr. Mac gives Sabrina a shot to sedate her. Next, as I hand Dr. Mac the tools one by one, she shaves the wound, cleans it with antibacterial soap, paints it with iodine, then sutures it up using a long needle and surgical thread.

I didn't think Ashley would be able to handle seeing Dr. Mac push the needle into Sabrina's skin, but Ashley is fascinated. "Hey, it's just like sewing," she exclaims. "We did that in preschool!"

Dr. Mac smiles. "That's right, it's exactly the same thing. And the skin will grow right back together where the stitches are." She gives Sabrina an injection of antibiotics and a tetanus shot, too, just to be on the safe side. Finally Dr. Mac stands up. "OK, keep her quiet for a few hours, and she should be good as new in no time."

Julie and her mother thank Dr. Mac. Then, to my surprise, they turn to me and start telling me how grateful they are. Julie's mother gives me a hug. I blush. *Sheesh!*

"Um, actually, the real hero is my little sister here," I stammer. "She's the one who noticed that Sabrina was crying."

Everyone turns to praise Ashley. "Someday,

you'll make a top-notch vet volunteer," Dr. Mac tells her. "Just like your big brother."

Ashley beams. Watching her tear-streaked face go from worry to joy, I know just how she feels. There's nothing like helping an animal to make you feel really good about yourself.

After we get home, Mom gives me a ride back out to the stables. Mr. Quinn has asked me to help him saddle a bunch of horses for a big trail ride.

As I walk over to the barn, Mr. Quinn calls out my name. I turn around, and he hands me a pitchfork. "You're going to need this first," he says with a grin.

I know, I know, I've gotta do my share of cleaning up after the horses. Not my favorite chore, but you can't exactly leave the stuff lying around in the horses' bedding! Mr. Quinn always says anybody can take riding lessons, but the true horsemen are the ones who care for the horses as well, all the way down to the last dirty detail.

So I shoulder my pitchfork with pride and head for the stalls.

That's when I see him.

He looks straight at me. "Hello, Son."

THREE

"Dad!"

Without thinking, I drop the pitchfork and rush to give him a huge hug. It feels great, it feels weird, it feels—I don't know what it feels like. Here I've just talked myself out of expecting to see him, and he appears in front of me. I'm not prepared for this.

The hug ends and we stand there, neither of us knowing what to say. I look at him, trying to see if he's changed at all.

He studies me the same way. "Overdue for a haircut," he says with a crooked smile.

I push my blond bangs out of my face and shrug. "Mom doesn't mind."

Dad opens his mouth to answer, then doesn't. He clears his throat.

Which makes me totally tongue-tied. It's strange to feel awkward around your own dad.

I'm relieved when Mr. Quinn strides over and breaks the silence. "Hey, Charlie, did you get to see the parade?"

"Caught a little of it," Dad says, but he doesn't say which part he saw.

Did he see me riding Trickster?

"You should have seen David," Mr. Quinn says, as if he's read my thoughts. He ruffles my hair, the way grown-ups do but shouldn't after you're about five. "Kid's pretty good with horses."

"He oughta be," Dad says—meaning, I guess, that I ought to be like him. I don't know whether to take it as a compliment or a criticism.

I look down at the ground, and Mr. Quinn clears his throat. Then he starts talking about the parade and horses some more, and the men laugh and talk as if nothing out of the ordinary was going on here at all. As if my father hasn't been gone for almost a year without even phoning his son.

"Mr. Quinn, Joe wants you," Zoe calls.

I turn to her, grateful for another interruption. "Hey, what are you doing here? They let you out of Intensive Care already?"

She comes over and holds up her arm. She has one of those super-wide Band-Aids on her elbow. "I'm fine. My camp instructor says you have to fall off your horse seven times before you're a real rider." She grins. "Only three more to go."

"Really?" I huff and shake my head, thinking of my dream and my fear of falling. "Maybe you can teach me how to do it sometime," I say under my breath so Dad won't hear.

Zoe just stands there making vague signals at me with her eyes. Oh, yeah—guess I better introduce her to my father.

"Zoe, this is my dad, Charlie Hutchinson," I say. "Dad, this is Zoe Hopkins. She works with me at the Wild at Heart clinic." I wrote to Dad about working at Wild at Heart, but he never answered. Maybe he never got the letter. If he did, does he remember? I can't tell from his reaction.

"Well, hello, Zoe, how are you?" He's all smiles, reaching out to take her hand, winking at me like she's my girlfriend or something. "Are you learning to ride, too?"

"Yes, sir," she says. Not yeah or uh-huh like most kids around here would say. She smiles politely and shakes my dad's hand. She's very sophisticated that way. Her mom used to take her everywhere in Manhattan, so she's used to talking with important grown-ups, like casting directors and chefs of fancy restaurants.

I can tell she's a little suspicious, though. Everybody at Wild at Heart knows about the situation with my dad, but Zoe probably relates to it more than anybody. Her dad split when she was really little, and she never hears from him at all. She says she doesn't really care. I'm not sure I believe that part.

"Well, I'd better get to work. It was nice to meet you, Mr. Hutchinson," Zoe says. "See you later, David."

Dad and I stand around awkwardly again. Trying to think of something to say, I blurt out, "Have you seen this horse, Dad?" I walk over to the stall where King's Shadow stands with his head out the door. His charcoal coat gleams as if he's just been groomed. "Isn't he awesome?"

Dad gives me a lopsided grin. "Glad you like him, son. He's mine."

I whirl around. "Yours? But he's been here since—" I don't finish the sentence. I don't say *yesterday*. I don't say, *What took you so long to come see me?*

Because I just realized, he *didn't* come here to the stables to see me. He came here to see his horse.

Now I feel really crummy and confused.

Then Dad says, "I've decided to move back to

Pennsylvania," as casually as if he were ordering a cheeseburger.

Suddenly it's like I've had the wind knocked out of me. I should be shouting hooray or something, but instead I feel scared. Scared of what? I'm not sure. Scared of getting my hopes up, I guess.

"Does Mom know?" I ask.

Dad looks away, shrugs, starts to speak—

Just then two minivans pull up, and a crowd of grown-ups and kids pile out. Mr. Quinn calls out my name.

The trail ride. I almost forgot why I'm here.

"Mr. Quinn needs me to help tack up," I explain to Dad. "Are you sticking around the stable for a while, or going over to the house?"

Dad shoves his hands into the pockets of his leather jacket. "Nah, I got a room at a hotel." The surprise on my face must show, because he adds quickly, "I got in late. Didn't want to impose on your mom . . . you know."

No, I don't know. Why wouldn't he want to stay in his own house, with his own family?

I don't want to think about what that means.

"David!" Mr. Quinn hollers.

Dad shoos me off. "Go ahead. Don't worry, I'll be here awhile," he assures me.

I head into the barn, and I have to admit I kind of welcome the distraction. It'll give me some time to get my head together about seeing Dad.

As I lead the last horse out of the barn for the trail ride, Mom and Ashley pull into the stable yard to pick me up. Boy, are they in for a surprise.

"Mom!" I call over the clopping hooves. "Guess what?"

I look around the yard for Dad. But I don't see him anywhere.

I search the barns and the practice ring.

My father has disappeared again.

FOUR

Here's one thing I'm always thankful for at Thanksgiving: we only have school on Monday and Tuesday, and the teachers tend to go easy on the homework. It's a good thing, too, because between bad dreams and worrying about Dad being in town, I'm not getting a whole lot of sleep.

Yesterday, all day long, I kept waiting for him to show up at the house or at least call us. But he never did. Mom said he probably had some business to take care of, but I could tell she was ticked that she hadn't heard from him. I mean, what kind of business would he be taking care of on a Sunday?

Today, when I go over to Quinn's Stables after school, my chores seem to fly by, even though I try to stretch them out as long as possible.

All too soon, it's time for my jumping lesson.

For years I've wanted to learn how to jump. But somehow everything has felt so unsettled this past year. And ever since my nightmares started, I've been afraid of jumping. Afraid of falling.

Sunita, who unlike me is a total brain at school, once explained to me where the word *nightmare* comes from: *mare* means not only a female horse, but also an evil spirit that haunts your sleep. Kind of funny in my case, since my nightmares are actually *about* horses.

Zoe, Maggie, and I saddle up for our jumping lesson with Mr. Quinn. Zoe takes Claiborne over the jump first, as Maggie and I watch from the center of the ring. Zoe's awesome—she doesn't just look like she knows what she's doing, she does it with style and makes it look so easy! She reminds me of the girl in this old movie, *National Velvet,* that she once rented for us to watch.

I study Zoe's every move, trying to figure out how she makes it all happen so smoothly, hoping some of it will sink into my brain. She's balanced in her seat, with a nice straight back (something I need lots of work on). She anticipates the jump perfectly and sails over the fence.

"Nice work!" Mr. Quinn calls out to her.

Zoe flashes a dazzling smile and canters to the

far end of the ring to walk Claiborne.

My turn.

I keep the picture of Zoe's jumping in my head as my horse, Comet, sets off at a walk along the outside of the ring.

I wish I were learning on Trickster. Maybe that would help, since Trickster and I are more than horse and rider, we're pals. But Mr. Quinn doesn't want him jumping yet, because Trickster still has some weakness in his leg from that trailer injury. Mr. Quinn is the kind of guy who doesn't take chances, especially with his horses, and he wants to make sure Trickster's injury is healed 100 percent.

So I've been learning to jump on Comet. She's an older horse, a little set in her ways but very smart, and we've been getting along pretty well.

"OK, David, let's see what Comet can do," Mr. Quinn says encouragingly.

I grip the reins and urge Comet forward while Maggie watches from the center of the ring.

As we move into a trot, Mr. Quinn calls out, "Too far forward, David." I scoot back in the saddle and almost slip. I shift forward again, feeling awkward.

"Settle down, David. Find your seat," Mr. Quinn says, as if I'm a beginner.

We start cantering around the ring, warming up

for the jump, and Comet tosses her head as if she too is getting impatient with me. Horses have a way of letting you know what they think of your riding.

I try to relax so that I don't send Comet the wrong message. "Good girl," I whisper at her long neck. "Everything's fine."

Comet listens to my body language, though, not my empty words. I try to encourage her to pick up the pace, but as we canter toward the jump, she's holding back. I can feel it. When we reach the jump, Comet balks, and I get ready for an awkward stop. Then she changes her mind at the last second and crow-hops over the jump. I hang on, but just barely.

I feel myself flush. This is really bad form! Comet snorts, as if even she's embarrassed. I sneak a glance at Mr. Quinn. The look on his face makes my heart sink. Disappointment.

"Let's try it again" is all he says.

I think I like it better when he chews me out.

We come back around and head for the jump again, even though I feel like calling it quits.

"You can do it!" Maggie calls out.

If she really thinks I can, she's the only one here who does.

I try hard to remember why I wanted to jump in

the first place. It seemed like a good idea at the time.

"If you feel Comet hesitate," Mr. Quinn says, "just give her a little kick."

I urge Comet forward, but she decides she can ignore a bad rider. *We're not going fast enough*, I think to myself as we approach the jump. But Comet heaves herself over, landing awkwardly, and I hang on like a dope. Compared to Zoe's movie-star grace, I must look like I'm in one of those funniest home videos you see on TV.

"Fine, David," Mr. Quinn says, even though his voice tells me he doesn't mean it. "Take a rest. Maggie, you're up!"

Feeling embarrassed and totally discouraged, I slow Comet to a walk and join Zoe at the far end of the ring.

"Don't worry about it," Maggie whispers to me as she rides past. I know she's trying to be helpful, but it only makes me feel worse.

Zoe's polite enough not to say anything. We ride side by side at a walk, cooling our horses. Suddenly Zoe points to the outdoor jumping arena near us. "Hey, look!"

A magnificent charcoal gray horse with a silver mane and tail stands tall in the center of the arena.

His rider swings into the saddle like some handsome lord of the manor.

It's Dad. On King's Shadow.

They walk and trot around the large arena, warming up. A handful of people gather to watch. My father sits in the saddle as if he's part of the horse, like one of those bronze statues where the horse and rider are melded into one piece of metal. There's no question who's in control.

Dad grew up on a horse farm in Kentucky. He learned to ride before he could walk, he says. And it shows.

Warmed up now, he and King's Shadow start jumping the course. The way they sail over the fences reminds me of the ice-skaters Mom likes to watch on TV, who leap effortlessly into the air, almost defying gravity, and land with such grace and flair. Each time Dad and King's Shadow nail a jump, I have to stop myself from bursting into applause.

I glance at Zoe. She looks impressed, too.

Dad finishes the course and calls out to Joe, who's been watching, and the stable hand runs out into the arena and raises the height of the fences. They were already high to begin with, but I can't believe the height Joe's setting them at now. Zoe lets out a low whistle.

Give me a break. No way that horse is going to make those jumps! He'd need a helicopter to get over them.

I wonder if everyone else is holding their breath like me.

Dad and King's Shadow take the first three jumps like champions. I exchange a grin with Zoe. Dad's amazing. He never misses!

Heading into the fourth jump, the biggest yet, King's rhythm seems off a little. But Dad's in control and presses forward with a look of determination.

They approach the fence, they jump—

Thunk! It's the sound all horse jumpers dread, the clunk of hooves hitting the crossbar.

The bar clatters to the ground. King's Shadow stumbles as he lands, but Dad stays glued in the saddle. As soon as King has collected himself, Dad reins him to a stop and dismounts to check his horse's legs.

Mr. Quinn runs into the jumping arena. "Is he all right, Charlie?" he calls.

"I think so," Dad answers.

Zoe lets out a deep breath. Slowly I let mine out, too.

King's Shadow shakes his head, as if he's trying

to shake the memory of that jump. Dad pats him on the shoulder and talks soothingly.

When Dad makes a move to remount, Mr. Quinn lays a hand on his arm. Dad whirls around, frowning. The two men talk, too quietly for us to hear their conversation. But we can hear the anger in their voices.

Maggie walks her horse over and joins us. "What's going on?"

"Dad wants to take the jump again."

"I don't think Mr. Quinn wants him to," says Maggie.

"Too bad. Because I know how this will end," I tell her.

Maggie looks surprised. "Yeah?"

"Yeah. Dad does what Dad wants."

Zoe's not so sure. "You know Mr. Quinn—he can be stubborn," she reminds me. "Especially when it comes to horses. Besides, it's his stable. Doesn't your dad *have* to do what he says?"

We wait to see.

Sure enough, a couple minutes later Mr. Quinn throws up his hands in disgust and walks away.

"Wow! I can't believe it!" Zoe exclaims. "He's totally ignoring what Mr. Quinn said."

I shrug. "King's Shadow isn't Mr. Quinn's horse.

I guess Dad doesn't care what he says."

Those jumps are killers. But my dad really is an awesome rider. I bet Mr. Quinn's jealous. He knows he couldn't have made those jumps. Probably he would have been too afraid even to try.

My dad's not afraid of anything. Unexpected pride flares in my chest.

Then again . . . I've gotten to know Mr. Quinn pretty well lately. He's tough but fair. He expects a lot from his riders, even the kids, and he's helped me become much more responsible around horses.

Maybe Dad should listen to Mr. Quinn.

Dad replaces the bar on the jump—same killer height—and swings back up onto King's Shadow.

Maggie glances at me. "Do you think he can make that jump?"

"Sure," I reply, but I'm worried. About what, I'm not quite sure . . . that Dad or his horse might get hurt? Or that they might embarrass themselves, and me, by not clearing the fence?

Dad gives King's Shadow a good long warm-up, taking extra time to check his stride. They look great together, a real team. Dad smiles confidently and pats King's neck, murmuring to him. The horse flicks an ear back to listen.

"I'm with Mr. Quinn," Zoe states. "I don't think

your dad should jump."

"He's a fantastic rider," I tell her. "He won championships when he was not much older than we are. You should see all his trophies. He was even on the 1980 Olympic equestrian team, but he never got to compete."

"Really?" Maggie says. "You never told me that! What happened? Did he get sick?"

I shake my head. Dad's disappointment was something I grew up hearing about a lot, especially whenever the Olympics were on TV. Dad would get this look on his face that was painful to see, because you knew how bad he was feeling inside.

"The whole American Olympic team had to stay home that year," I explain. "The United States boycotted the Olympics. There was some kind of stupid political argument with Russia or something."

"Wow." Even sophisticated Zoe is impressed.

"Yeah, well, that tells you how good my dad is."

We fall silent as Dad goes for the first jump. King's Shadow lifts his tail like a flag and picks up speed. Man, he's gorgeous when he runs.

Dad takes him over the first jump like nothing has happened. King's Shadow seems totally at ease. Horses respond to a confident rider, Mr. Quinn always tells me. I can sure see that happening here.

Then Dad skips the second and third jumps.

Huh? Is he bagging it?

No, he's going straight for the fourth jump—the biggie.

Zoe turns away. "I can't watch."

I lean forward, my heart pounding. I can't *not* watch.

I cross my fingers. *Do it, Dad. Show them!*

King's Shadow leaps—and soars over the jump.

"They made it!" I shout, shaking my fists in the air. *Way to go, Dad!* I gaze after them in admiration as they canter by, King's silver tail streaming like a banner.

Wait a minute—is King's canter a little off? No, it can't be, he's fine. And yet . . . I squint, watching his legs as he runs.

"King's limping!" Zoe exclaims.

Sure enough, the limp becomes more and more obvious. King is clearly favoring his right foreleg.

Now Dad realizes it, too. He pulls King's Shadow to a stop, then slips off to check.

The look on Dad's face tells me it's not good. I turn to Zoe and Maggie. "I think King's Shadow is hurt!"

FIVE

Maggie, Zoe, and I watch as Dr. Mac examines King's Shadow. The horse stands cross-tied in the aisle of the barn, remarkably calm and unfazed by all the fuss. Dad slowly strokes King's shoulder. I glance quickly at my dad. I'd be totally ashamed if I'd just done what he's done, but his face is unreadable.

Mr. Quinn's mouth is set in a hard line. Nothing makes him madder than people who foolishly endanger a horse.

"We'll need X rays of the leg," Dr. Mac says, giving us kids a meaningful look. We go out to her van, unload the portable X-ray machine, and carry it back to the barn. It's about the size of a toaster oven.

Dr. Mac and Mr. Quinn put on large lead-lined aprons and mittens. I've worn those before, and they're heavy. The lead blocks the radiation from the X rays.

Then Dr. Mac slides a thin metal case about the size of a large book into a wooden box. That's the X-ray film. She hands the box to Mr. Quinn, who positions it behind King's right foreleg.

"Everyone else, get back," Dr. Mac orders. She aims the lens of the X-ray machine at the injured leg and pushes a button. She takes a couple more X rays from different angles, just to be sure.

When she's done with the X rays, she examines King's leg one more time, her hands moving gently as she glances up at the horse for any reaction. Then she has Dad walk him back and forth while she watches his limp, frowning.

"I'll look at the X rays back at the clinic," she says at last, "but I'm pretty certain that there's no fracture."

"Thank God!" Mr. Quinn says under his breath.

Dad doesn't say anything. He just looks relieved.

"However," Dr. Mac adds as she begins to wrap King's foreleg in a bandage, "there could be a serious stress injury. If he's been doing a lot of jumping, you should take him to the equine clinic so they can do a force-plate analysis."

"What's that?" I ask.

"It's a test performed on a special treadmill that measures the force each leg is putting down when the horse walks," Dr. Mac explains. "The force-plate analysis reveals the degree of weakness in the injured leg, and it helps us plan his physical therapy more accurately."

Mr. Quinn stands up with his hands on his hips and slowly shakes his head at my dad. "Operating on people-time, Charlie?"

Dad presses his lips together and glances away.

"What's people-time?" I ask.

Dad doesn't answer. Doesn't even look at me. I'm not sure he even knows I've spoken.

"People-time is the hurried pace we humans live by," Mr. Quinn tells me. "We worked by horse-time when we got Trickster used to the trailer again. Remember how long that took?"

Do I! "Forever," I answer. Every day we led Trickster a little closer to the trailer, sometimes only a step or two closer and only for a few minutes. It was tedious, and I got pretty impatient. I thought Mr. Quinn was being ridiculous. But he was determined to do it that way, taking baby steps. This went on for weeks.

And then, bit by bit, Trickster began to lose his fear of the trailer. Finally, we had him happily eating his breakfast right in the trailer! Mr. Quinn sure knew what he was doing, and I really admired his patience when I saw how well it worked.

"You know, Charlie," Mr. Quinn says to my dad, "you can't force a horse onto people-time. He was not ready for that jump. Now he can't jump at all."

"How bad do you think it is?" Dad asks quietly.

Dr. Mac turns and studies my father's face like she's trying to read an X ray. "Only time will tell," she says. "Horse-time."

Dad can't hold Dr. Mac's intense gaze. His eyes lower, and that look of confidence he always has evaporates. In fact, he looks miserable. He knows it was all his fault.

Boy, do I know how that feels.

"Hungry?"

I've just finished my chores around the barn, and suddenly Dad is standing there, leaning up against the barn door as if he just happened to be there and I just happened to walk by.

"Always," I say.

He chuckles. "That's the way I was at your age. Never could get enough to eat." His smile fades a little but doesn't disappear. "It's all that growing you're doing," he adds softly.

Have I grown? Do I look different to him? I don't feel any different since he left, at least not on the outside.

"Why don't you call your mother and tell her you'll be home after dinner," Dad says. "We can go get a bite to eat."

"Have you seen her yet?" I blurt out.

Dad looks at the nails on one hand. "I stopped by her office today, but she was out with a client." He pauses. "She seems to be doing well there. Nice office." He sounds almost surprised. Surprised that she's doing well without *him?*

I almost say, *It's a good thing, because we need the money.* But I don't want to spoil the moment.

Dad hands me his cell phone, and I call Mom. "Hi, Mom, it's David. Um, Dad's here. He wants to take me out for something to eat."

Mom doesn't say anything for a second. Then, "Your father's there? At the barn?"

"Yeah," I say lightly, trying to make it sound normal that he's been to the stable but not to his own house. "He says he came by your office today, but you were out." I hold out the phone to him. "You want to talk to her?"

He steps back, not expecting that. Then he looks

at his watch and waves a hand. "We'd better scoot."

I stare at him. Is my dad afraid to talk to my mom?

"David? Are you there?" Mom asks.

"Oh, yeah, Mom. So can I go?"

"Sure, I guess so," she says. Not *Where is he staying? Is he coming for Thanksgiving dinner? Let me talk to him.* Nothing. We let it go at that.

We climb into Dad's car—actually a small truck that's seen better days.

"What happened to your SUV?" I ask him.

Dad snorts as he pulls out onto the road. "Guy ran into me. Totally wrecked it. I got it fixed, but it was so messed up"—he shrugs—"I just sold it. A friend let me have this to drive, just till I figure out what I really want to get." He pats the dashboard. "Gets pretty decent mileage, for a truck. And it hauls anything."

We drive along, not talking much. At last we pull into the parking lot of Taco Bell. It used to be our favorite place to go. It's been a long time since we've been here together.

We go in and order, loading up two trays with all our favorites. Then we slide into a booth and dig in. There's a lot of "This looks great!" and "Yeah, here, want some of this?" We stay busy unwrapping straws and rustling papers and chowing down so we don't have to talk.

The silence is heavy with all the things we aren't saying. I slurp down some soda and shift in my seat.

Dad leans back and wipes his mouth with a paper napkin. He takes a little sip from his drink, then shakes the cup, rattling the ice.

Finally he says, "I'm really looking forward to Thanksgiving dinner." Just like any dad who hasn't been gone for a year.

Some kids might say something mean at this point. But when I look Dad in the eye, I can't. He actually seems kind of sad to me. Maybe this has all been hard on him, too. Maybe he wants to explain.

Maybe he wants to come home.

"Yeah," I say. "Turkey and stuffing, mashed potatoes, pumpkin pie—Mom's going all out."

Dad nods. "Your mom's a good cook."

"Except for when she gets on a health-food kick!" We laugh. Suddenly it feels great to be with Dad after so long. "So what have you been up to?" I hope it's OK to ask.

"Oh, you know . . ." He stirs a chip in a puddle of nacho cheese sauce. He talks about what he's been doing, but he's kind of vague. It sounds like he's traveled some and has been "really, really busy." I don't get any specifics. Soon he steers the conversation toward something we both like: horses.

"Quinn told me about you and Trickster," Dad says. "Sounds like a fine horse."

"He's awesome!" I tell him. "My riding's really improved, too. But jumping—man, that's a lot harder than it looks."

Dad leans forward. "What you need is a teacher who understands you. Quinn is good, don't get me wrong. But he's a little . . ." He searches for the right word. "Easygoing. You know? Slow-paced. You'll never get anywhere if he doesn't push you a little. You have to challenge yourself in order to grow, David. That is, if you really want to be a champion rider."

"I do!" I insist.

Dad smiles at me with a strange look on his face, one I can't quite read. "I remember that first time I put you on the back of a horse." He laughs. "Your mom just about had a fit! I was afraid she was going to call the authorities."

"How old was I?"

"About ten months old."

"You're kidding!"

"You grabbed right on, though," Dad says. "I was

so proud of you! I told your mom you were a natural."

Proud of me? A natural? My heart leaps over a hurdle.

"I have high hopes for you, David. You've got the talent; you just need a little more fire. But I expect you'll be riding a real jumper—like King's Shadow—in no time." He wads up some food wrappers and stuffs the ball into his empty cup. "Say, how would you like me to give you some jumping lessons?"

Would I! "Really?" I exclaim. "That'd be great, Dad! You're the best rider I've ever seen!"

He smiles the biggest smile I've seen since he got here, one that goes all the way up to his eyes. "You're on!" he says. "What do you say we start tomorrow—meet at the stables after school?"

"You bet!" I tell him. It's an offer I can't refuse.

SIX

When we get home that night, Dad pulls up to the curb but keeps the motor running.

"Aren't you coming in?" I ask.

"Sorry, David, I've got some important calls to make."

"But what about Ashley? She's dying to see you!"

"I'm going to see her tomorrow, I promise," he insists.

Yeah, right. I climb out of the truck.

"It'll be a surprise for her!" he adds lamely. "And tell your mom I'll call her."

As I walk in the door, Mom looks up expectantly, but when she sees I'm alone, her face quickly goes blank. I deliver Dad's message, and she nods. Then she puts me to work polishing the silver for the big Thanksgiving dinner she's planned.

She's invited Dr. Mac, Maggie, and Zoe to join us, plus a few people from her office. So we're all working like crazy to get everything ready. Despite all the work, I can tell she enjoys the hustle-bustle of holiday preparations.

Right now she's making her special cranberry relish while Ashley works at the table beside her, coloring name cards for our guests. Brian is bringing in firewood to have ready for Thursday. Even I start to feel cheerful and excited about the holiday, in spite of my worries over Dad being here.

Brian dumps his load of wood by the fireplace in the family room, then turns to Mom. "Do you need any more stuff from the store? I can swing by on my way home from work tomorrow."

Mom beams at his thoughtfulness but shakes her head no. "I've got everything I need," she says with satisfaction. And as she looks around the kitchen at me and my brother and sister, I think maybe she's not just talking about ingredients for the meal.

Wiping her hands on her apron, Mom leans over and kisses Ashley on the top of her head. Everything feels peaceful and contented, kind of like in one of those holiday commercials for stuffing.

I just hope nobody changes the channel.

When I get to the barn after school the next day, Dad's waiting for me. He grins at me, and I smile back. It's starting to feel like it used to. Not nervous, the way you feel around company. As if we're remembering how to be together.

At first it feels just like the old days, when Dad used to give me lessons. He seems really happy to be here with me, and it feels wonderful to have all his attention like this.

He watches as I trot around the practice ring on Comet.

"Tighten up your reins a little, David. That's right—let the horse know you're in charge."

I adjust my reins for more control, then press Comet into a nice, steady canter. I'm trying hard to please Dad. At least my seat feels balanced for once, like I'm moving *with* Comet, not just *on* her.

"Looking good out there!" Dad calls. "Keep that up, and you'll be in the 2008 Olympics!"

My heart swells in my chest, and I feel almost as if I could fly. *I'm so glad Dad's back!* I tell myself to quit worrying so much about him. Everything's going to work out fine.

"It's time for Air David to take flight," Dad announces with a grin. But instead of setting up the practice jump, he walks to the far end of the ring and opens the gate to the big outdoor jumping arena. "You might as well start learning on a real jumping course."

I'm not sure I'm ready for this, but I take a deep breath and follow him into the arena.

Dad must have caught my look of doubt. "Lesson number one: act confident, even if you're not, to psych out the competition," he tells me with a wink. "Don't worry, Comet's jumped this course before. She'll show you how it's done."

Despite Dad's encouragement, I can't help feeling nervous about the jumps. My lesson yesterday was a total disaster, and I don't want to repeat that in front of Dad. But I'm his son, I remind myself. I must have *some* of his talent.

Dad sets the jumps low, and Comet takes them with no trouble at all. It's actually kind of fun going over one jump after the other, getting into a rhythm. When we finish the course, I'm feeling good, but tense. The sweat from my palms has soaked through my riding gloves. *You can do it, David,* I tell myself. *Make Dad proud of you.*

"Hey, kiddo, you're making this look too easy!" Dad says with a smile, raising the crossbars higher. He's setting them nearly three feet off the ground, higher than I've ever jumped before.

He's testing me. Challenging me. Comet watches Dad with interest, her ears perked forward.

I want to take that challenge, but something holds me back.

"I—I'm not sure we should try those yet," I say.

Dad stands with his hands on his hips, feet apart. "Are you afraid of the height?"

"No!" I swallow. "But Comet needs to build up to that height," I try.

Dad's eyes bore into mine. "Trust me, son. That horse *wants* to go over these jumps. Look at her— she's champing at the bit! These jumps aren't that high, to a horse. But of course you can't do it if you tell yourself you can't. Come on, give it your best shot."

What am I supposed to do—say no?

I take a deep breath, press my heels to Comet's sides, and point her toward the first jump. My nightmare flashes across my mind, and I fight to send it packing. Can't think about that now.

Comet speeds into a canter, but her strides are short and jerky. My heart sinks—she can tell I'm nervous.

When we reach the first jump, her stride is totally off, and she swerves around the jump instead of leaping over.

"Whoa!" Dad hollers out.

I pull Comet up and glance at Dad. He's got the look of someone who's good at something and impatient with those who aren't.

"Sorry, Dad. Comet just wouldn't go over," I try to explain, cringing at the whine in my voice. Dad hates excuses.

He shakes his head. "Comet's not the problem, David. Never blame your horse." He sighs. "This is where Quinn would simply lower the bar, and your mother would probably tell you to quit and go home." He looks me straight in the eye. "But I know *you're* not a quitter."

I try not to flinch under that commanding blue gaze. I want to say, "Come on, Dad. Let's go play mini golf or watch a football game—anything but jump!"

But I can't. Not with that look on his face. He wants to believe in me—to believe that his son is a champion in the making. I can't let him down.

"Right," I say loudly, trying to force some confidence into my voice. I adjust my helmet, wipe my gloves on my pants, and turn Comet back around for another try.

We halt for a moment while I stare at the jump. Dad once told me that Olympic athletes use mental imagery to help them nail a performance. A gymnast might visualize a little movie in his head of himself running, leaping, hitting the vault, twisting high in the air, then sticking the landing. That's what they're doing when you see them on television just standing there, staring at the vault before they start to run.

So I picture myself and Comet cantering in perfect rhythm, flying over the fences together, landing smoothly like pro jumpers . . . Dad beaming proudly as I ride up to the winner's circle. *That's my boy!* I imagine him saying.

OK. I'm ready.

With a new burst of determination, I approach the first jump again, focusing on my vision of success. *Go, go, go!*

Against my will, my pathetic jumps from yesterday suddenly fill my mind, and my confidence seeps away with each hoofbeat as we draw closer to the jump. I feel as if I'm on a runaway train, heading for disaster—and I don't know how to stop.

I can't do this! I'm going to make a fool of myself in front of Dad!

Comet senses my fear—I can feel the change in her gait. Right before the jump, she ignores my feeble kick, plants her hindquarters, skids to a halt, and sends me flying through the air like a catapult.

And then I fall, fall, fall . . . just the way I do in my nightmare.

Only this time I know it's for real.

I hit the ground—*oof!*—and lie there, wondering why I can't seem to breathe.

SEVEN

When I wake up, I'm not sure where I am.

In bed, having one of those dreams?

My shoulder hurts, and I groan.

A high-pitched whinny splits the air. Trickster? The fog in my head slowly clears. No—it's Comet.

The jump . . . we fell . . . Comet must be hurt!

I struggle to sit up, but strong arms hold me down. I taste blood in my mouth. A gentle hand brushes the dirt from my face.

I squint, trying to see. Faces come slowly into focus. My father is on one side of me, Mr. Quinn on the other. Both of them look strangely pale. Their voices are calm and soft. "Don't move," they tell me. "Lie still."

I clutch at Dad's sleeve. "Comet—is she OK?"

Dad's face nearly crumples. "She's fine, son. I promise. I'm sure you are, too."

Promises.

A siren shrieks. Lights flash as an ambulance arrives. My eyes drift closed. Man, my head hurts.

When I wake up, I'm in a hospital. Darn! I always wanted to ride in an ambulance, and here I went and slept through the whole thing.

They wheel me into the emergency room. I've never been in a hospital before, except to see Mom when Ashley was born. All the nurses and doctors seem to be rushing, but calmly, like they've seen it all before and know what to do. It reminds me of being at Wild at Heart, the way Dr. Mac moves so quickly when she's got an animal in trouble . . . I remember all those sick puppies, we had to work so fast . . .

My eyes drift shut.

When I open them again, the nurses and technicians hover around me, setting me up for X rays. It hurts like crazy when they move me into different positions. I mumble something about Dr. Mac's portable X-ray machine being a lot easier on the patient, and they look at me like I've gone off the deep end.

Then they wheel me into a little room, where I

wait awhile. Finally, a young doctor comes in. "Good news, bud," he tells me. "Nothing's broken. You're just a little banged up."

"That's good," I whisper.

"Yes," he says, "you were lucky." He pats me lightly on the arm. "Be prepared for some major bruises, though. You'll be pretty sore for a few days."

The doc helps me up off the table—*umph!*—and leads me out to the waiting room. My parents are sitting there with strained faces, not talking or looking at each other. Several Styrofoam coffee cups litter the small table between them. I wonder how long I've been here.

Dad looks up and spots me. "David!"

Mom jumps to her feet and rushes toward me, her eyes brimming with tears. Dad is right behind her. They throw their arms around me.

"Ouch!" I yell before I can stop myself.

"Oh dear, did I hurt you, sweetheart?" Mom asks, stepping back.

"No, no—I'm fine." I try to smile. "Just kind of bruised all over."

It's the truth, but not the whole truth. Seeing them together like this, I realize how much more I'm hurting on the inside than on the outside.

Dad turns to the doctor. "How is he?"

"He's all right, considering. Pretty banged up, but nothing broken. I'll give him a prescription for painkillers if you want. But I think ibuprofen should take care of it."

"What about all the blood that was on his face?" Mom asks.

"Just a nosebleed," the doc explains. "Always looks scarier than it is." He scribbles something on a prescription pad and hands it to Mom. "Call if he has any dizziness or nausea. But I expect he's going to be just fine." He smiles at me. "Take care and get some rest—and stay off those horses for a few days!" He turns to go.

"Thanks, Dr. Michaels," Mom says, dabbing at her eyes with a tissue.

I glance up at my parents. Dad's face is pale and tight, and Mom looks positively sick with worry.

What can I say? "Sorry, Mom, sorry, Dad. I totally blew that jump," I mumble.

Mom's never been all that wild about me riding horses. Unlike Dad, she doesn't ride at all, and she's always been fearful that I might get hurt, especially once I started jumping. Now I'll probably never even get to *see* another horse as long as I live, much less learn to jump.

"I'm really, really sorry," I say again.

Mom glares at Dad and then bursts into tears. Dad looks really uncomfortable and clears his throat a few times.

This is totally weird. How come they're not getting on my case? How come Dad's not telling me how badly I messed up?

And then I hear the strangest thing. Dad is apologizing—apologizing to *me*. "God, I'm so sorry, David," he says. "It's all my fault."

I blink, suddenly feeling dizzy. "*Your* fault? But—"

"I was stupid," he says harshly. "I pushed you too hard, too fast. You never would have tried that jump in a million years if I hadn't pushed you to do it. I—I just wanted—" He holds out his hands helplessly. "I'm sorry." He turns to Mom. "I'm so, so sorry."

I look at Mom. She's so angry with him she's about to explode. I can tell because she's real quiet. But then she takes a deep breath and her face softens a bit. "Well, Charlie, I'm glad you got him to the hospital so fast. And I appreciate you calling me right away so I could be here when you arrived." She turns to me and smoothes my bangs out of my eyes. "Now, let's get you home and into bed."

Dad swallows. "Right, that's a good idea." He squeezes my hand. "I'll see you tomorrow, son. All right?"

Somehow I have the feeling he's asking Mom for permission as much as he's promising me he'll be there.

EIGHT

When I wake up the next morning, I get a clear picture in my mind of the life-size plastic skeleton model in Mrs. Nelson's science class.

That's because I can feel every bone in my body. I shift positions and find a couple more bones I forgot I had.

Then I notice a little munchkin standing beside my bed, wearing a purple sundress over a turtle-neck and tights. Ashley stares at me, her eyes as round as saucers. Finally she whispers, "Are you still alive, David?"

"Yeah," I answer. "You guys aren't getting rid of me that easily."

Her eyes get even bigger.

"I'm just kidding, Ash!" She looks so worried, I open my arms for a hug.

She hugs me very, very carefully, as if she's

afraid that I might break.

So what can I do? I just *have* to tickle her!

She shrieks in delight and jumps out of my reach. "Mo-om!" she screams, giggling.

That's better.

"I brought you some breakfast," she announces and carefully picks up a tray that she has set on the floor. She carries it over at an impossible angle. I hope some of that juice makes it all the way over to me.

I take the tray. She's made very, very dark toast with about a half a jar of strawberry jelly mounded up in the center of it. "Thanks, Ash. It, uh, looks delicious."

"Can I have a bite?"

I hand her half the toast, and she happily stuffs it in her mouth.

I remember then that it's Wednesday—no school today. That's a relief. And Mom's taken the day off work to get everything ready for Thanksgiving tomorrow.

Something flies through the air and lands with a thump on the bed right next to me. What in the world?

It's a tube of sports cream. I look up to see Brian standing in the doorway. "This stuff is mostly useless," he says, coming over to sit on the edge of the bed, "but maybe it'll help those aches and pains a little. At least the smell will keep the girls away."

I laugh. "Thanks."

"Heard a horse tried to play Frisbee with you."

I shrug. I don't want my big brother to think I'm a wimp. "They say you have to fall off a horse seven times before you're a *real* rider," I tell him.

"Really? Man, and I thought football was hard!" Brian says. It's almost as if he's impressed.

Suddenly the doorbell rings and Ashley jumps, dropping jelly toast down the front of her dress.

Her eyes light up. "Maybe it's Daddy!"

"Ashley, wait!" I say.

But she's already flying out of the room.

Brian's eyes lock with mine. He knows Dad's back in town. Mom hasn't told Ashley yet. I guess Mom's been waiting, to make sure he shows up.

"Have you seen Dad yet?" I ask Brian.

Brian shrugs, his face a mask. "Nope. And I don't particularly want to."

"Brian, he's moving back to Pennsylvania!"

"Yeah, right. Keep dreaming, kiddo."

"No, I mean it, he says he's moving back," I insist. "I think he's trying to . . . I don't know, make things better."

Brian looks down at me, and I'm shocked by the

raw anger suddenly revealed on his face. "Well, maybe things are better the way they are."

"Brian! How can you say that?"

"Easy. I've got things worked out just fine, thank you. I've got a job, friends—I've got a life, man. Who needs him?"

"Daddy!" Ashley squeals from the front hallway.

Brian turns his head, listening for a moment. Then he jumps up off the bed. "I'm outta here."

"Brian, wait—"

"Hey, I've got to get to work," he says. "Do you know how many cute girls show up at the movies when there's a school holiday?"

And he's out the door. I hear him greet Dad briefly in the hallway, as if it's just another day, and then the front door slams. Brian's gone.

I throw back the covers and dress as quickly as I can, but I'm so stiff and sore that it's a painful process. I'm groaning and pulling a T-shirt on over my head when I hear footsteps on the stairs, and suddenly Dad's standing there in the doorway. Ashley's holding on to his hand, smiling like she's going to burst.

"See? I *told* you it would be Dad!" She looks up at him and heaves a big, exaggerated sigh. "He *never* believes me."

Dad and I laugh. Then I notice Dad's holding something—a big box with a large orange bow on top. He hands it over and I rip off the lid. "Sweet!" It's a fancy new riding helmet with a bright green Lycra cover. "It's excellent, Dad. Thanks!"

"Well, you put a few dents in the old one," he says. "Can't have you riding around in a banged-up helmet. What would the horses think?"

I smile and try it on. "How do I look?" I ask Ashley.

She cocks her head, twirling a finger in her hair. "Kind of like Kermit the Frog," she decides.

We all laugh, and then I notice Mom in the doorway, watching, a half-smile on her face.

"Did you see my new helmet, Mom?" I ask.

Mom nods. "Very nice. Looks expensive," she adds.

Dad shifts from one foot to the other, then quickly says, "I was thinking of taking Ashley out for a bit."

Mom hesitates, as if it's something she wants and fears at the same time. She doesn't want Ashley hurt. But at last she says, "Sure, why not. Only—" She peers more closely at my sister and shakes her head. "My goodness, sweetheart!" Ashley has strawberry jelly all over her face and down the front of her dress. There's even some in her hair. "We'll have to get you cleaned up first. Come on, missy, you need a bath. I hope I can get that jelly out of your dress."

"I'm not taking it off!"

"Oh yes you are, young lady."

"Do as your mom says, pumpkin," Dad chimes in. "I'll wait. You look so pretty in that dress—don't you want it washed so you can wear it tomorrow for Thanksgiving?"

Ashley nods and dashes for the bathroom, and Mom gives Dad a grateful smile.

I try not to be jealous of all the attention Ashley's getting from Dad. After all, I had him to myself yesterday. But still, I can't help wishing I were the one he was taking out this morning.

Then I have an idea. "Hey, Dad, while you're waiting for Ashley, want to see the animal clinic where I volunteer? It's just across the street." I want Dad to know I'm not a total failure at everything. Maybe he'll be impressed when he sees what I do at Wild at Heart.

"Well . . ." He looks back over his shoulder. "Ashley will be ready soon—"

"It'll only take a minute. Come on . . . Please?"

"All right, David. Sure, let's go."

"I'll bring Ashley out when she's ready," Mom tells us.

Dad and I walk across the street to the clinic. "I work over here several hours a week," I explain. "Like I told you about in my letter."

"Terrific," Dad says. "How much do you make?"

"It's volunteer work, Dad."

"Oh." Dad nods. "Well, that's good, too."

When we walk in, the waiting room is empty of patients. Maggie and Zoe are at the front desk, looking for something in Dr. Mac's overflowing pile of papers.

Dad says hi to Zoe, and I introduce Maggie. "This is Maggie MacKenzie, Dr. Mac's other granddaughter." I turn to the girls. "Are Brenna and Sunita around?"

"Not yet," Maggie says, munching on a muffin. "Things are pretty slow today, anyway."

"Want one of these?" Zoe offers a plate of muffins. "Cranberry-orange. I just baked them this morning."

I grab two—I never did eat the half jar of strawberry jelly on charcoal toast that Ashley brought me for breakfast. And Zoe is a great cook. She says the housekeeper who raised her taught her how to make everything. Before Zoe moved in, about the only things Dr. Mac and Maggie ate were cold cereal and frozen pizza.

Dad starts to sit down on one of the chairs in the waiting area, but I tug him back up. "Come on, I want to show you around."

We head back toward the examining rooms. "Dr. Mac named her rooms after veterinarians from favorite books," I explain. "This is the Herriot Room. And this one's named after Dr. Dolittle."

Just then Dr. Mac comes out of the Dolittle Room with a broom and dustpan. I cringe a little. Here I'm hoping to show Dad what a fast-paced medical clinic this is, and Dr. Mac's playing janitor!

"Good morning, David. How are you feeling?" Dr. Mac inquires.

"What's wrong?" Zoe and Maggie ask at once.

I guess they haven't heard yet. "Well, my dad was giving me some jumping lessons. I cleared the jump perfectly. But my horse stayed behind."

Everyone laughs.

"Look on the bright side," Zoe says. "Only six more falls to go."

"Well, feel free to look around, Mr. Hutchinson," Dr. Mac says. "Maggie, would you mind going upstairs and getting the folders that are on my nightstand?"

"Sure, Gran." Maggie hops up and heads through the door that connects the clinic to their house.

Dad looks around politely. I wonder if he's bored. I sure wish something would happen so he could see what we do here.

Dr. Mac turns back to my dad. "It's not usually this quiet around here," she explains, as if reading my mind. "Guess it's the holidays. I'm actually enjoying the lull for a change. Gives me a chance to get caught up on my research." She chuckles. "That is, I *was* getting caught up, until my modem threw a tantrum. Now I can't get on the Internet at all."

"Don't look at me," I say. "That's Sunita's department."

She nods. "I keep telling myself I'm going to take a computer class. I guess I'll have to add Sunita to my Thankful List."

"Your what?" I ask.

"Just what it sounds like—a list of all the things I have to be thankful for."

You'd think Dr. Mac has the perfect life. She gets to work with animals. She loves what she does, and everybody loves her. And she even writes a column for the newspaper. But she's had her share of hard times. Maggie's parents, her own daughter and son-in-law, died when Maggie was little. And from what I can tell, she doesn't even speak much with Zoe's mom. So now she's raising two granddaughters *and* running her clinic.

"So I write a Thankful List every November," Dr. Mac continues. "It helps me stay focused on all the good things in my life, not on what's going wrong at the moment."

"Sounds like something we could all stand to do," my dad is saying, just as the door flies open and a woman rushes in.

"Dr. Mac—Omar is choking!" Andrea Moore, a young woman who lives a few doors down, holds up a large Siamese cat that's making horrible gagging noises. She's got the cat wrapped in a towel to protect herself from scratches, but he's almost clawed his way out.

Everybody moves into action. Clutching Omar, Andrea follows Dr. Mac into the Herriot Room.

"Hands!" Dr. Mac calls over her shoulder.

We know what that means. Even in an emergency Dr. Mac insists on clean hands. We wash up while Dr. Mac swipes the stainless steel examining table with an antiseptic.

Andrea lays her cat down on the table and carefully removes the towel. Omar coughs and wheezes as Dr. Mac begins her exam. First she runs through the basics—she checks Omar's pulse rate, gently presses his abdomen, and looks for signs of injury.

I have to admit cats aren't my favorite animal. I'm much better with dogs (and horses, of course). But I can't help feeling sorry for this poor cat. He acts as if he can barely breathe.

As Zoe and I hold Omar still for Dr. Mac, I glance over my shoulder. Dad is standing just outside the doorway. I guess he doesn't want to come in and be in the way. He shoots me a thumbs-up. I'm glad he's getting to see me at work. Now I just hope we can save this cat.

"Did you actually see him swallow something?" Dr. Mac inquires, gently opening the cat's mouth and peering inside with a penlight.

Andrea looks embarrassed and pushes her wire-rim glasses up on her nose. "No, but I found part of my Thanksgiving turkey on the floor," she admits.

Uh-oh. Omar could be choking on a bone.

Dr. Mac just nods, calm and businesslike, and sets Omar on his feet. He stretches his head and neck forward in this really freaky gagging position and coughs hard, over and over. It's scary.

How can Dr. Mac stay so calm?! "Do you think it's a bone?" I ask her. "Maybe the Heimlich maneuver would help."

"Cats almost never choke," Dr. Mac says. "The opening to a cat's windpipe is very small and closes instantly. And you can't do the Heimlich maneuver on cats. But I suspect this is something else. He's in a great deal of respiratory distress."

Andrea looks frantic. "Can you help him?"

Dr. Mac nods. "David, get the O_2. Small mask. Zoe, check his respiration rate."

I roll the canister of oxygen next to the table and turn it on, then hook up a small mask to the tubing.

"Pulse rate is 240 per minute," Dr. Mac reports. "His heart's racing. Respiratory rate?"

"It's hard to tell with the coughing," Zoe replies, "but I'd say about 50 breaths a minute."

I don't need a veterinary degree to know the cat is breathing way too fast.

Dr. Mac starts adjusting the dials on the oxygen machine. "Go ahead with the mask, David."

I've watched Dr. Mac do this lots of times, and it always looks easy. But it's hard to put something over an animal's face when it seems to be choking to death. I feel my own heartbeat and respiration rate go up as I slip the small mask over Omar's tiny nose. He twists and turns a little at first, trying to shake off the mask, but stops fighting when the oxygen begins flowing into his lungs.

The poor little guy—he's shedding fur all over the exam table. Cats do that when they're really frightened.

"Nice job, David," Dr. Mac says quietly. "Now help Zoe hold him still—but gently." I slip my hands onto the cat's heaving sides as Dr. Mac turns to open a cabinet behind her.

I wonder if Dad is still watching from the hallway, but I've got my back to the door and can't turn to look.

"It's OK, Omar," Andrea croons to her cat, kissing his paw. "You're going to be all right."

Seconds later Dr. Mac is back at the table, a needle and syringe in her hand. "I'm going to give Omar some medication. Hold him still for the injection." She positions the needle and presses the plunger in one smooth motion.

"New pet?" Dr. Mac asks as she discards the needle.

Andrea nods.

"How old is Omar?"

"We think he's about three," Andrea says. "We just got him from the pound a week ago." Her lip trembles a little. "We think he's a purebred Siamese. I can't believe somebody gave him to the pound!"

Dr. Mac doesn't answer. She's seen far worse things happen to animals than just being given to the pound. She glances at Zoe. "Make a note that I administered fifty milligrams of prednisone sodium succinate."

"Got it," Zoe says, recording the dosage in her neat handwriting.

Dr. Mac peers closely at Omar, watching to see how he responds to the medication. "Have you noticed any symptoms of illness since you got him, Andrea?" she asks.

Andrea bites her lip and thinks for a moment. "Well, he's been sneezing a little, off and on, but I've been kicking up quite a bit of dust, cleaning for company." She pauses again. "And he hasn't been eating all that much. I thought maybe he was just getting used to his new home. You know how finicky cats can be."

Gradually Omar's breathing slows, and he begins to look more relaxed and normal.

"What did you give him?" Andrea asks.

"A fast-acting steroid. Seems to have gotten him past this attack."

Andrea frowns. "What do you think was wrong with him?"

Dr. Mac runs a hand through her short white

hair. "Well, I want to run a few more tests—some blood work, a chest X ray, and a chemistry profile. Plus a routine heartworm check, just to rule out everything else," she says. "But I suspect Omar has asthma."

"Asthma!" Andrea says. "I . . . I didn't know cats could have that!"

"It usually occurs in cats between the ages of one and eight," Dr. Mac explains. "Females are twice as likely to develop the condition, but males can get it too. And guess which breed appears to get it more?"

"Siamese?" I ask.

Dr. Mac smiles. "Bingo."

"But he seemed fine when we brought him home from the pound," Andrea says. "Why did he get so sick all of a sudden?"

"The attack may have been caused by something in his new environment," Dr. Mac explains. "Hair spray, cigarette smoke, even household cleaners . . ."

"Well, I have been cleaning like mad," Andrea says, then frowns. "My brother's here, too, for Thanksgiving, and he's started smoking again."

"Any or all of those things could have triggered a bad attack like this," Dr. Mac says.

"Oh, Omar, I'm so sorry," Andrea says, cuddling the cat to her chest.

"The good news is that asthma in cats can be treated, just as it can be in people," Dr. Mac says. "Omar seems to have responded well to the steroid injection. So, unless the tests turn up something different, we'll probably get him on prednisone and see if that helps his symptoms."

"Thank you so much, Dr. Mac," Andrea says. "All of you—I'm sure you saved his life just now."

I turn to look for Dad and—*crash!*—knock over a tray of instruments.

Zoe giggles, but she kneels down to help me. Dr. Mac just looks mildly amused. It's not the first time I've done this, and I know she's not mad.

Still, I'm embarrassed to have messed up again in front of Dad. As I scramble to pick up the instruments, I glance out into the waiting room to see if he's still watching. But he's not there.

Brushing cat hair off my pants, I go to the door and look around the waiting room, then up and down the hall. I don't see him anywhere.

I can't believe it. He left again, without even saying good-bye.

NINE

Opening the clinic door, I check outside. Maybe Dad left because of the choking cat. Some people just can't stomach medical emergencies. Besides, maybe he's had his fill of emergencies in the past two days.

Sure enough, when I step outside, there's Dad across the street, leaning against his truck, talking on his cell phone. I heave a sigh of relief. He didn't skip out. And he didn't leave because I embarrassed him. *Get a grip, David!* He just had to make a call. He probably wanted some privacy, or maybe the phone reception's better out here.

Ashley is already sitting inside the truck, so excited she's bouncing up and down.

Dad's got his back to the clinic and doesn't see me coming over. As I cross the street, I catch part of his conversation.

"A job like this in Philly would be perfect," he says.

My heart jumps. He's really moving back—he really does want to be near us!

I pause by the tailgate. I know I shouldn't eavesdrop, but I can't help listening in. I mean, this is *my* life he's talking about, too.

"Listen, Isaac," Dad is saying, "is there any way you can find out for me? I really need this job . . ."

Isaac? That must be his friend Isaac Jackson. They've been good friends since high school, and I know Mr. Jackson works at a company in Philly. I take a step closer, straining to hear.

". . . hasn't been easy since I got fired . . ."

I freeze in my tracks. *Fired? Dad got FIRED?*

"No, I haven't told anybody," Dad says, kicking at the truck's front tire. "I want to keep it quiet . . ."

I can't believe what I'm hearing.

Ashley knocks on the window, telling Dad to hurry up, and he looks up and calls through the glass, "Just one more minute, pumpkin."

". . . I know, I know," he says, speaking into his cell phone again. "I appreciate that, Isaac, but I'm in emergency mode here. Unemployment doesn't even begin to cover my bills . . ." He's pacing in front of the truck now, rubbing his forehead with his free hand. I duck behind the tailgate. "OK, OK," he says, "but when do you think they'll decide?"

The pieces of the puzzle are beginning to fall into place, and I'm getting a pretty good idea of the big picture. Dad came back here *not* because of me and Ashley and Brian and Mom. And he's not some big-time business guy who's so busy that he doesn't have time for his family.

No—Dad came back to beg favors from old friends, because he got fired from his job in Texas! Sounds like it happened a while ago, too. Is that why he got rid of his expensive SUV and drives a beat-up old truck?

It also explains why Dad stopped sending Mom money—he doesn't have any. I think about the new riding helmet he gave me and get a sick feeling in my stomach. How did he manage to buy that? And how could he spend money on a luxury like King's Shadow when he's having trouble paying his bills?

I don't care about Dad's money. Or what kind of car he drives. Or whether he has a fancy horse or buys me presents. I just want him back, just want us to be a family again.

But Dad lied to me! He's only moving back to Pennsylvania because he needs work. Not because he misses us.

Ashley presses her lips and cheeks against the truck window, making goofy faces, trying to get Dad's attention. My stomach twists, and I want to run and scoop her up in my arms to protect her.

Suddenly I feel just the way I did in the dream, and the way I felt going over that jump with Comet. As if I'm falling, falling . . . then hitting the cold, hard ground with a thud. As if all the breath has been knocked out of me.

I can't believe what a chicken my dad is—he's too scared to tell me the truth.

Dad clicks off his cell phone and slips it back into his pocket. He still doesn't see me.

I'd better not let him know what I've heard.

No! Maybe the old David would have done that. It would be easier, less painful to pretend I don't know anything.

But I'm too mad to just let it go. As he reaches to open the driver's side door, I step out from behind the truck. "Dad—wait!"

Dad turns around, surprised, then gives me one of his charming smiles. "David! Hey, how's the cat doing?"

It must be the look on my face that stops him cold. He tries again. "Hey, that was pretty neat the way you guys saved that cat. Sorry I had to slip out.

I needed to check my phone messages at the hotel—"

"Coward!" I blurt out.

Dad's jaw drops.

Did I really just call my father a coward? I don't care. All this time *I've* been so afraid of looking like a coward in his eyes, because I'm afraid of falling off a jumping horse. Now I realize that's nothing to be ashamed of compared to what *he's* done.

"David," he says, holding out his hands, palms up, like a criminal trying to look innocent, "what are you talking about?"

I step closer and stare straight up into his startled blue eyes. "You're afraid to admit why you're really here!"

"What do you mean?" he asks.

I glance at Ashley inside the truck. The windows are rolled up and I try not to shout, so she won't hear me. But it's hard, because I'm so mad I'm shaking. "You think you can just turn up after a year? Just pop back into our lives like nothing's changed, bring a pretty horse, be the big shot again?"

"David—"

"Ashley cried for months when you left!" I hurl at him. "We *all* missed you, Dad. You stopped calling. You didn't even write." I pause to fight down some angry tears. "Mom knocks herself out to look after us and pay the bills, too. And Ashley—she wears that stupid purple sundress all the time like it's some magic princess dress that will bring you back if she just wishes hard enough. Brian won't talk about you at all. Don't you care how much you hurt us?"

Dad looks like a statue for a moment. Or a handsome mannequin posing as a dad in a department store window. Then he takes a step toward me, his hands outstretched. "I don't know what you heard, David, but I can explain—"

"Don't bother." I start to turn away.

Dad's strong hand comes down on my shoulder to stop me. *Ow!* He doesn't even remember how sore I am from the fall. "David," he says again, his voice husky. "Wait."

Don't, I tell myself. *Just keep going. Keep going until you're so far away, you can't hear any more of his lies.*

But Dad doesn't let go. Slowly I turn around, daring him with my eyes to lie to me again.

Dad's shoulders slump, and he looks tired. "You have to believe me, David. I know I messed up." He looks at me, silently pleading for me to understand.

I don't say a word.

"I *have* been trying to get a new job in Philly," he admits, "but it *is* so I can be closer to you and Ashley and Brian. That's why I was asking Isaac Jackson for help. He might have a lead on a good job—"

"Yeah, right."

"It's true!" he insists. "Listen, there are a lot of other places I could look for work—and places where I could probably make more money. But I don't want a job anywhere else. I know that now."

I stare at him through narrow eyes.

"I miss you, David. I miss my family, more than I ever could have imagined. But . . ." He jams his hands into his pockets and rocks on his feet. "I know it's going to take time before you trust me again."

"Horse-time," I interject.

"Not that long, I hope!" Dad jokes lamely.

I don't even crack a smile.

"David, please—hear me out!" He gazes down at my face, begging me to listen. "I love you, son," he says hoarsely. "I love all of you. It's just that . . ." He runs a shaky hand through his thick blond hair. "Lately everything has been kind of confusing."

"Tell me about it," I retort. "Couldn't be as confusing as it is for Ashley."

Dad winces. "OK, I deserve that. But, David, try to understand—"

Enough of his weaseling excuses. I cut him off. "No, thanks. I'm not really interested anymore." I turn around, and this time I'm really going.

"David!" Dad calls after me. "We'll talk some more . . . tomorrow. After you calm down."

I whirl around. "Forget it, Dad! Don't even bother to come. We don't want you at our Thanksgiving dinner—because you're the last thing we're thankful for this year."

TEN

I run up the driveway and grab my bike from the garage. Hopping on, I pedal furiously toward the stables. My bruised body feels every tiny bump in the road, but I don't care. Nothing hurts as badly as the way I feel inside.

I pedal harder and reach Quinn's in record time. Tossing my bike down on the gravel, I head for Comet's stall. I realize I forgot my new riding helmet, but I don't even want it now. I'll just wear my bike helmet.

I don't need Dad to teach me how to jump. I don't need Dad for anything. I don't need that fancy new helmet, and I especially don't need his show-off horse—a horse he bought with money he should have sent to Mom.

Mr. Quinn doesn't seem to be around, but he's told me I can ride Comet on my own. I brush and saddle her, breathing in her comforting horsey smell. Then I fling myself onto her back and take off.

Comet doesn't question or judge me, just goes willingly where I ask. Instead of turning into the ring, I ride away from the barn, past Mr. Quinn's big stone house, past the duck pond, and along the edge of a green pasture until I pick up a trail. Comet seems glad to be out of her stall, and once she's warmed up I let her stretch out and run. It must be great to be a horse and just run because it feels good, instead of being driven by fear and anger.

We gallop and gallop along the edges of fields and up a big hill. Comet breaks a sweat and I can feel her sides heaving, but she doesn't slow down. I lean low over her neck and feel myself become part of her rhythm.

Gradually my anger burns off, and the wind in my face seems to blow away some of the pain. Finally, as it starts getting dark, I turn back to the stables.

I take Comet through the jumping arena on our way to the barn. The white stripes on the jumps seem to glow as the world shifts from color to shades of gray. The whole place is eerily quiet, deserted.

I rein Comet to a stop, and we stand there,

looking at the jumps. Comet's ears flick back and forth as she waits, trusting me, waiting for me to tell her what to do.

I'll show Dad. I'll jump and jump and jump till I can do it. No matter how many times I fall, I'll get up again and keep jumping. Maybe I'll even try out for the Olympics someday—and I'll actually win!

That'll show him.

I kick Comet in the sides, and we start toward the first jump.

Comet seems slow, unsure maybe, so I turn her around and we start over. I have to do it just right.

"Let's go, Comet, what are you waiting for? We can do this!" I say. "Come on, girl, don't quit on me! What's the matter—are you afraid?"

Comet lowers her head and nibbles at a piece of hay on the ground.

Then I realize what I just said.

I sound just like my father.

I let the reins fall slack. I'm not going to jump this horse. She's tired and hungry. It wouldn't be safe, not for me or for Comet. I'd just be pushing her to try to prove something to myself—and Dad.

The memory of my father jumping King's Shadow flashes into my mind. What was *he* trying to prove?

I pat Comet on the shoulder. "Sorry, girl," I tell her. "You deserve better." Then I slide out of the saddle and lead her toward the barn. She deserves some dinner and an extra-good grooming.

Suddenly I notice a man silhouetted in the light of the barn, watching me from the doorway.

Oh, no. I really don't want to see Dad. Not now. Not yet.

I look away, but I force my feet to keep walking forward. I'm not going to run away from him, the way he ran away from us when the going got tough.

As I get closer, I look up—and realize that it's not Dad. It's Mr. Quinn.

"Hey," I say.

"Want some help with Comet?" he asks. "Looks like you gave her quite a workout."

He doesn't press for an explanation, so I just shrug. "Sure."

We cross-tie Comet in the grooming stall, and I fetch the grooming kit—hoof pick, brushes, comb, and towel. Using the pick, I clean all the dirt and gravel out of each hoof, watching Mr. Quinn out of the corner of my eye. His hands are practiced and sure as he brushes the sweat from Comet's coat, and the horse seems to enjoy his firm, gentle touch. My hands aren't as experienced, but I hope

Comet can tell how I feel through them anyway.

I finish up with the hooves and move to the mane and tail. I spray on a detangler and then work slowly, using a comb and my fingers to get rid of all the tangles. Mr. Quinn takes the towel to give Comet's coat a final polish.

After we finish, we check on King's Shadow and Trickster. Both of them have some healing to do, and I know Mr. Quinn will make sure it's on horse-time, not people-time.

I feel like Mr. Quinn's using horse-time on me, too, the way he lets me learn slowly, bit by bit.

And he's using horse-time now as he waits for me to say what's on my mind.

I lean over the door to Trickster's stall and breathe in the rich smell of horse and hay. To me it's the best smell in the world.

"I found out why Dad really came back," I find myself saying.

"Oh?" Mr. Quinn picks a piece of straw off his plaid shirt.

"Yeah. He got fired from his job out in Texas. The only reason he's back is that there's a friend here who can get him a job." I swallow back a sob that's trying to form in my throat. "Didn't have anything to do with us."

Mr. Quinn clears his throat. "Yes, I knew he'd lost his job."

"You did?" I exclaim.

Mr. Quinn nods. "I thought your father should tell you about it himself. Wasn't my place."

I guess I can understand that. "I don't think I can ever forgive him for lying about the whole thing," I confess as Trickster comes over for some petting. I stroke his nose, enjoying the velvety feel of his soft muzzle. "I used to think Dad was the greatest. But not anymore."

Mr. Quinn raises his eyebrows, but he doesn't speak.

"In fact," I continue, "I don't want to be anything like him. I'm even thinking about giving up jumping. Who needs it? It's just for show, anyway."

"Well," Mr. Quinn says, gazing at Trickster rather than me, "I hope you won't do that, David. As much as you may not want to hear it, you do have your father's gift with horses. Only you have an advantage."

My head snaps around in surprise. "Advantage? Like what?"

"Unlike your dad, you don't have anything to prove."

I suddenly think of Dad watching the Olympics

on TV—how sad and kind of bitter he always looked. He used to say he'd give anything for a chance to compete. The Olympics were supposed to be his big moment, but he never even got there.

"Of course, you can also be stubborn and impatient like him, too," Mr. Quinn says with half a grin.

I start to protest, but I know it's true. "I don't want to be anything like him," I bite out.

"We can't help being like our parents in some ways," Mr. Quinn says. "But you just showed that you're also different from your father. Like just now, when you didn't jump."

I glance sideways at him, a blush creeping up my neck. I stuff my hands down into the pockets of my jeans. "So you saw me."

He nods. "I watched the whole thing. You've got a lot of love and respect for these animals, David. You've also got good intuition—when you stop and listen to it." He turns and smiles at me. "You don't have to prove anything to anybody but yourself. If you remember that, you'll not only be as good a rider as your dad—you'll be better."

I'm stunned speechless. The blush has totally taken over my whole face and head. Finally I manage to stammer out, "Thanks a lot, Mr. Quinn. I—I mean it."

I think of Dr. Mac's Thankful List and realize that maybe I should start one of my own. Because I'm awfully thankful for Mr. Quinn.

As we head out of the barn to lock up, he says, "I'll let you in on a little secret, though."

"What?" I look up at him.

"Your dad's just human, like the rest of us. Even if sometimes he likes to act otherwise." Mr. Quinn chuckles as he flicks off some of the lights. Then his face turns serious again. "He really does miss you kids. And you know why he's working so hard to find a good job?"

"'Cause he needs the money?"

Mr. Quinn smiles. "Because he wants you to be proud of him."

ELEVEN

I go home and do something that I think will
make Mr. Quinn proud of *me*.

I call my father at his hotel.

"David," Dad says, sounding surprised.

I take a deep breath. "Forget what I said about
tomorrow," I blurt out.

Dad waits.

"Ashley will be really upset if you don't come to
dinner."

"Think so?"

"I know so. And you know what else, Dad?"

"What?" His voice sounds hopeful.

"You gotta be there—'cause Mom's not so hot at
carving the turkey."

Dad laughs out loud. He wasn't expecting that.
Then he gets quiet. "Do *you* want me there, too,
David?"

I squeeze the phone receiver in my hand. I don't know how to answer.

How I feel about my dad has changed so much in the past two days. It's gotten a lot more complicated. I don't know if I'll ever be quite as proud of him as I used to be. But he's still my father. The only one I've got. And as Mr. Quinn says, he's only human, just like the rest of us.

"Yeah, Dad," I say simply. "I do."

"I'll be there," he says.

And, this time, I believe him.

The next morning, Mom's running around like a crazy woman trying to get everything ready—and loving every minute. The turkey smells great, and I can't wait to sit down and dig in.

Finally Dr. Mac, Maggie, and Zoe arrive. With Mom's friends from work plus me, Ashley, Brian, Mom, and Dad, we can just barely squeeze around our dining-room table. The table is all dressed up with Mom's best china and crystal, stuff she doesn't even let us touch the rest of the year. She's even put candles in the middle of the table, along with some flowers that Dad brought over.

Mom brings out the turkey and carves it herself,

and guess what? She does a darn good job. Dad winks at me, and I hide a smile.

Once we've all filled our plates and begun eating, Mom tries to get everybody to go around the table and tell something they're thankful for. Brian and I roll our eyes at each other—it's so hokey! But she always likes to do this sort of thing on holidays.

Dr. Mac starts by saying she's thankful for her Wild at Heart kids—that's us! Ashley says she's thankful for her purple sundress (as if we didn't know). One of Mom's coworkers, who just moved here from Laos, says she's thankful to be having a real American holiday.

When they get to me, I blurt out, "I'm thankful Zoe brought black-walnut chocolate cake!" And soon everyone's laughing so much, we never make it the rest of the way around the table.

I glance at Dad and wonder what he might have said. He looks pretty happy to be here, so maybe I can guess.

Zoe cuts into the cake and insists on giving me the first big slice. Mom's beaming, and Dad looks relaxed. I even catch Brian talking with Dad. I can't hear what they say to each other, but Brian's eyes seem to lose some of their hardness.

I think it's easier for Dad having lots of other

people around. He and Mom seem to be getting more comfortable with each other as the meal goes on. Not like lovey-dovey or anything, but pleasant.

Watching them, I realize they probably won't get back together. That makes me sad. But I realize that I'll never really know what they've been through as a couple. I guess we'll all just have to figure out this new way of being a family as we go along.

Oh yeah, I almost forgot—when Dad showed up at the door, he told us that he'd nailed the job in Philly. I also saw him slip an envelope into the pocket of Mom's apron. I think I know what's in it.

After all our guests have left and the sun is getting low, Dad stands up, patting his stomach, and calls out, "Anybody up for a little touch football?"

I look at Brian. He and Dad hold each other's gaze with matching blue eyes. I know Dad's asking him more than just that simple question.

In an instant, I can tell Brian's going to ruin it. He's going to say no and bolt.

I rush over and punch my brother on the arm. "Hey, Brian. Let's play."

I can see Brian is torn. I know how he feels.

"Come on," I badger him. "Scared you're gonna lose?" Then I add so quietly that no one else can hear, "Please?"

Brian hesitates, then shrugs. "OK, OK. Why not?" He punches me back and shoots a grin at Dad. "Beats cleaning up the dishes."

"Not so fast!" Mom says, pretending to be mad. "You're not getting off that easy." She holds out her arms, as if to prevent our escape.

Brian shoves his hand out, like he's blocking for me, and we dodge around her, whooping and hollering.

"The dishes will be waiting when you come back in!" she assures us.

"I wanna play, too!" Ashley shouts, tagging along.

Dad scoops her up. "You can be on my team," he says, swinging her up onto his shoulders as she shrieks with delight.

We dig the football out of the garage and head out into the cold November afternoon.

High Hurdles

By J.J. MACKENZIE, D.V.M.

Wild World News—Horses are natural jumpers. With their large, muscular hindquarters and long legs, they can propel themselves over jumps taller and longer than they are. But carrying a rider over a jump is another matter. To avoid injury, both horse and rider must be carefully schooled in the art of jumping.

Whether you're a beginner or riding for ribbons—or even if you just love watching jumping from the comfort of your couch—there's plenty to learn about this thrilling sport.

Jumping ABCs. The first obstacle a horse and rider learn to go over is not a jump at all, just a series of poles lying on the ground. As the horse

trots over each pole, he won't have to jump, but he will have to pick up his feet carefully and pay attention to what's in front of him—good preparation for jumping.

Continued on page B14

Thanksgiving Parade Attracts 20,000 People

Continued from page B7

Next, the rider takes the horse over a low jump. As the horse rises into the air, the rider stands slightly in the stirrups and leans forward to help the horse over. Gradually, as the horse and rider develop greater skills and confidence, they work up to higher and higher jumps.

Staying Safe. How safe is it to become airborne on top of a 1,000-pound animal? Like all sports, jumping has risks. That's why a rider should always wear a well-fitting riding helmet. Traditionally, "hard hats" are made of cork covered with black velvet, but now they're sometimes made of hard plastic with foam inside, much like bike helmets. (In fact, some helmets are dual-certified for biking and riding.)

protective boots

For taking higher jumps, horses sometimes wear their own safety gear. Special guards, or "boots," can be fastened around the horse's lower legs to help prevent bangs or bruises if the horse hits the crossbar.

Even the jumps are specially designed with safety in mind. They are brightly painted, usually in white and a contrasting color, so that the horse can 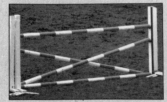 see them clearly. Horses see only in black and white, so having light and dark colors makes the jump more visible against the ground. And all but the most advanced types of jumps are designed so that the crossbar will fall off the hurdle easily if the horse hits it, which reduces the risk of injury.

Showtime! For centuries, riders have enjoyed jumping horses over fences, streams, and logs while racing cross-country. This kind of racing became known as *steeplechasing*, because the riders often used church steeples as landmarks to guide them through the countryside. Now-  adays a steeplechase means a full-speed horse race over a

steeplechase

large course with extremely difficult jumps—not for the faint of heart! If you've seen the classic movie *National Velvet*, you have a sense of how

Continued on page B17

Continued from page B15

challenging this sport can be. The race that young Velvet rides in (dressed as a boy, since female jockeys weren't allowed!) is the most famous steeplechase in the world, an English race called the Grand National.

Show jumping, another type of competitive jumping, takes place in show rings or arenas. Show jumping has been an Olympic event since 1900. As with steeplechasing, riders must clear the jumps in a certain order or they're disqualified. But in show jumping, the horse and rider must also avoid being penalized for mistakes, or *faults*. Each rider jumps the course one at a time, with the judges watching closely. The rider is faulted if the horse knocks the bar off the jump or balks at a jump and refuses to go over. Three refusals in a row and you're out! If two or more riders tie for first, they jump the course again. Then the rider with the fewest faults *and* the fastest time wins.

HORSES CAN CLEAR JUMPS AS HIGH AS SEVEN FEET.

Beginning jumpers can enter *schooling shows*, small local shows for less experienced riders. At these shows, different classes have

schooling show

jumps set at different heights to suit riders of varying levels. Speed is not important, so the riders are not timed. Instead, the goal is to jump the course smoothly and cleanly, showing good form, with as few faults as possible.

The Sport of Champions. You can watch the best jumpers in the world on television, competing in the Olympics and other international events. You'll  see an impressive variety of difficult jumps, such as walls, water jumps, and *combinations* in which horses must go over two or three jumps one right after the other. You'll see horses clearing heights of seven feet or more and jumping over obstacles that really do look impossible! ✦

Ambler Girl Wins State Jumping Competition

About the Author

Laurie Halse Anderson has had many pets—dogs, cats, mice, even salamanders—but never a horse. She has ridden a few, though. One summer, she went on a trail ride. Suddenly, her horse spooked and bucked hard. Laurie was really scared, but she stayed in the saddle. Good thing, too, because just then, a mama black bear and her two cubs came out of the trees, and Laurie had to get out of there in a hurry!

Laurie has written many books for kids, including an award-winning young adult novel, *Speak.* When she's not writing or teaching writing workshops at local schools, Laurie splits her time between bird-watching and hanging out at the local vet clinic. She lives in Ambler, Pennsylvania, with her husband, her two daughters, and a cat named Mittens.